Praise for Julian Iragorri and Lou Aronica's
The Edge of the World

"A fascinating character study that digs deep into individuals in different eras but tied together by the colors emulating from others."
— Genre Go Round Reviews

"Like eating a fresh lime sorbet with saltwater in your (sex-tousled) hair."
— Smallgood Hearth

"Reminds us how intricately we are all tethered together."
— Lazy Day Books

"One of those books where you can't stop reading. It was an amazing read and I think you should give it a try."
— Ruby's Books

BIRTH RIGHT

BIRTH RIGHT

JULIAN IRAGORRI AND LOU ARONICA

THE
ST●RY
PLANT

The Story Plant
Studio Digital CT, LLC
PO Box 4331
Stamford, CT 06907

Copyright © 2019 by Julian Iragorri and The Fiction Studio, LLC

Print ISBN-13: 978-1-61188-266-7
E-book ISBN-13: 978-1-945839-29-0

Visit our website at www.TheStoryPlant.com
Visit Lou Aronica's website at www.LouAronica.com

First Story Plant printing: September 2019
Printed in the United States of America

To my daughter Olivia, who made my life.
— J.I.

To everyone who tries.
— L.A.

"We have two lives. Our real life and a second life in the memories we leave behind"
— Told to Julian by Eigen Onishi, a Buddhist monk at the Kiyomizu-dera Temple in Kyoto on March 10, 2017

Chapter 1
New York, USA, February

Alex Soberano always awakened five minutes before his alarm went off. He didn't need to look at the clock on his bed stand to know that it was 5:25 a.m. when he'd opened his eyes. This never varied more than a minute in either direction. Alex often considered the possibility of not setting the alarm at all, since he hadn't awakened at any other time in years, even Sundays, but he still toggled the device on every night. No reason to leave something to chance when avoiding an inconvenience was so easy. He switched off the clock so it wouldn't awaken his wife, kissed Angélica's shoulder (knowing that this wouldn't wake her but would elicit the slightest sigh, a sound he adored), and got out of bed.

His home office was on the other side of the apartment, across from the living room. It had once been in the third bedroom in the sleeping wing, but Alex moved it when he discovered that his daughter Allie was such a light sleeper. He couldn't even type an email without hearing her stir. She needed her sleep, so disrupting her in the slightest way wasn't an option. And the forty-fourth-floor view of Central Park from the study was nicer in the morning, anyway.

Alex sat in his office chair, handmade by an artisan from Anhelo, the South American city where his great-grandmother Vidente had lived. It was Alex's souvenir from the trip he'd taken there with Angélica and Allie two years earlier to introduce his daughter to the land of her forebears. When the artisan learned that Alex was a descendant of the great Vidente, he begged Alex to commission a work, saying he would do the job at an enormous discount just knowing that Vidente's great-grandson would be sitting in something he'd made. Alex found the man's passion — not to mention his idolization of a woman who'd died more than ninety years earlier — moving, and he engaged the artisan in a discussion about his work. Once they came to an agreement on the specifications for the chair, Alex insisted on paying full price. People with a genuine commitment to what they were doing deserved remuneration; the world was hard enough for them already, even though the world would be forfeit without what they did.

Alex responded to some email messages from Asian partners. There was nothing terribly challenging in any of this correspondence. Asian markets had been stable for a few years now, and Alex's biggest initiative in that region — a cooperative with a pair of tech savants from Vietnam — was at least a half-year from beta testing, so this morning's catch-up was little more than letting everyone know that, as always, he was around and available if something should come up.

The correspondence with the Europeans was different, though. There was so much wariness about the "loose cannon" that had been elected prime minister in Léon, and this crept into nearly every message, even from those who'd always shunned politics and those who had no business holdings in that Western European country. It was a bit like the overheated exchanges he witnessed immediately after Brexit. If Romeo Ólgar wanted to make his presence felt quickly in the European Union, he had accomplished that mission. Léon — and much of Europe, for that matter — had seen their share of overreaching leaders over the years. Unlike in other parts of the world, though, it had been a long time since any of those despots had proven to be more than a nuisance and an embarrassment. Ólgar sounded boorish, but he probably wouldn't turn out to be any worse than, say, Berlusconi had been in Italy, not that he wished anything like Berlusconi on his friends in Léon. Of course, if he turned out to be like Mussolini — and Alex had to admit there was a certain Mussolini-like message in Ólgar's proclamations — then all of the concerns of his European compatriots would be more than justified.

Alex probably wouldn't have given it another moment's thought if it had been any country other than Léon. He had connections all over the continent, but Léon was special, both professionally and personally. From the fact that Legado, the country of his birth, was once a colony of Léon (and Alex spoke the language like a local), to Alex's business interests there, to his deep affection for the royal family, that nation had a special place in his heart and mind. It was still difficult for him to understand how the good people of Léon had elected someone as mean-spirited and tone-deaf as Ólgar, but one could hardly be surprised by any election anymore.

Alex took a moment to respond to a particularly troubled email from a Spanish associate:

> Chin up. Your country survived Franco. Ólgar
> will turn out to be nothing more than a pim-
> ple on Léon's beautiful face.

Then he sent a couple of quick before-you-get-to-the-office notes to some of his New York staff and browsed his favorite news sites. At 7:30, it was time to wake up Allie.

Alex entered his daughter's room and kissed her softly on the forehead. This, of course, was enough to awaken her, and she uncurled slowly before tossing off her covers. Getting Allie ready to go to school every morning meant getting to the office later than he ever had previously, but he cherished this time alone with her. Given the nature of his days — and, increasingly, hers, as academics and extracurriculars took more of her time — these were likely to be the only peaceful moments they'd have together until the next morning. He was not about to miss them.

He made himself an espresso while he waited for Allie to come to the kitchen. As he took his first sip, inspiration struck, and he walked to his daughter's bathroom door.

"Pancakes?" he said.

"Really? Do we have time?"

Alex did a quick calculation. He'd made her pancakes on a school day in the past, but he'd always started the batter before awakening her.

"Sure. As long as you're completely dressed and packed up."

"Yeah, that would be great."

Alex walked back to the kitchen briskly. First true objective of the day.

As he put some butter into the microwave to melt, he remembered that he wanted to drop his dear friend Fernando, the crown prince of Léon, a note about planning a family dinner when he was in town in a couple of weeks. The Ólgar thing must have prompted that reminder. He'd take care of that before going to the office.

For the next half-hour, though, it was all about Allie. And the pancakes.

◊ ◊ ◊

Colina, Legado, South America 1992

Alex had been to exactly one inaugural ceremony before. His parents had taken him to see President Marcador take the oath of office back when he was thirteen. That president had turned out to be ineffectual, serving only one term and, even at his young age, Alex had the sense that Marcador was going to be a footnote in Legado history. The man projected so little presence, almost as though he didn't have enough internal energy to put a persona out there. What Alex subsequently learned was that Marcador was a compromise candidate during a period of transition for his country. The story would be decidedly different sixteen years later, when a wildly charismatic candidate — one who happened to be Alex's cousin — would take the nation by storm and win the election in a landslide.

Alex could hardly believe the ceremony he was watching today had the same function as the one he'd witnessed as a boy. This one had so much pomp, so much music, so much color. Javier Benigno was easily the most popular political figure to rise from Legado since the late, ever-beloved Viviana Emisario, and perhaps the first to inspire the passion from the people that seemed to have been extinguished when Viviana's helicopter had crashed during a diplomatic mission. Viviana's death had snuffed the joy from a nation. It had done more than that to Alex, but that was a story he would forever keep to himself.

"Legado was always our most vibrant colony," said a voice to his right. "This ceremony has more hues than a Joya de la Costa garden."

Alex turned to look at the speaker. The man seemed to be about his age and height, though he was a bit heftier all around. *Maybe this is what I'd look like if I didn't spend as much time in the gym,* Alex thought.

"I assume you're aware that Legado hasn't been a colony since your great-great grandfather was a twinkle in his mother's eye."

The man flashed a heavy-wattage smile. "Oh, well, of course. But one never stops thinking of their children as children, do they?"

"Well, we're all grown up. And we've been a democracy continuously for more than a century. I don't believe our 'father' can say the same thing."

"I don't know what you mean," the man said, laughing boisterously. "The public elected El General to each of his nine terms. By an overwhelming majority, in fact. Usually more than ninety percent."

A huge cheer went up at that moment. Looking down from the grandstand, Alex could see that the new president's motorcade had entered the staging area.

"Yes, ninety percent," Alex said to his companion. "My cousin should find that humbling, as he only received fifty-nine percent of the vote."

"Cousin? I assume that makes you a Benigno."

"Soberano, actually. Javier is a cousin on my mother's side." Alex put out his hand. "Alejandro Soberano. My friends call me Alex."

The man shook. "Fernando Alfonso Trastámara. My friends call me Fernando."

Alex should have recognized the man. He'd certainly seen the heir to the Léon throne in enough tabloids. "They don't call you 'Your Majesty.'"

"God, no. They will hopefully never call me that."

"I assume that means you're wishing for a very long life for your father and not that you're expecting El General to come back from the dead."

The man beamed again. It was easy to see why women found him so irresistible. Between the smile, the future crown, and the massive fortune, what was there to resist? "No, El General is gone forever. Just to make sure, my father sends an envoy every day to dance on his grave."

Alex nodded approvingly. The people of Legado did indeed consider Léon to be close family, and the last thing that Alex would have ever wanted was a return to the days when El General dominated Léon so absolutely. Alex was barely in elementary school when the dictator had suddenly stepped down, allowing Fernando's father, Juan Alfonso Trastámara, to take his rightful place on the throne and to allow for a duly elected prime minister to operate the government, but he could remember his mother spitting invective at the television every time she saw El General speak. And while Alex didn't truly understand the cause of celebration on the streets of his hometown when El General resigned (and the only slightly-less-raucous celebration that happened when the dictator died eight months later), he would never forget the taste of the *pastel con tres leches* his mother made that night to mark the occasion.

"Very wise of your father," Alex said. "Is he here?"

"He wishes he could be. He thinks highly of your cousin. But there's a gathering of several European heads of state that Léon is hosting, so he of course needed to attend that. He sent me to represent the crown in his stead. He's accurately deduced that my one statecraft talent is waving and smiling broadly, so I'm the perfect man for this assignment."

Fernando did some smiling and waving at that point and excused himself. At the inaugural ball that evening, though, Fernando came up to Alex with two glasses of Champagne and offered him one.

"I noticed you didn't have a drink," he said.

Alex took the glass and tipped it in Fernando's direction before taking a sip. "I was pacing myself."

"I don't have the remotest idea why anyone would do that."

Alex grinned at Fernando's acknowledgment of his excesses. "Lots of family around. And I wouldn't want to do anything that might embarrass my cousin."

"Hmm. Interesting perspective."

"It was nearly time for another drink, though, so I appreciate the Champagne."

"Happy to be of service. So, I hear you've been conscripted to accompany me to Anhelo tomorrow for the hospital ribbon-cutting ceremony."

Just a few hours earlier, Alex had learned that his cousin, the president, had requested that Alex be part of the prince's travel party for the opening of a new hospital that Léon had funded. The request had surprised Alex, because he'd never performed any sort of official government function before, and there were surely dozens of people on the presidential staff who could have filled this role. Had someone seen Alex and the prince speaking at the inauguration and decided that Alex would be a good companion? He did notice his mother looking at them a lot during the inauguration and then he saw her talking to the president later. Maybe she wanted him to become friends with the prince? But he doubted she would have such influence on the new president, even though he was her younger cousin. Did President Benigno think this might help groom Alex for some future place in his administration — something Alex had never considered and wouldn't particularly desire, especially now that his career was kicking into its next gear? Regardless, he wasn't going to turn down the new leader of his native land, and some pomp and circumstance at the side of the prince of Léon could be entertaining.

"Yes," Alex said. "It appears they needed to tap the absolute best available talent for this engagement."

"I'm flattered. I was afraid I was going to get a member of Benigno's rotund retinue. Is it just me or is everyone in the president's inner circle at least forty kilos overweight?"

Alex chose not to respond beyond a polite smile.

"No matter," the prince said. "Tell me: is the Colina after-hours club scene as ribald as its reputation?"

"I wouldn't really know. I'm down from New York, and I grew up in Anhelo. I've never taken much advantage of the clubs when I've been to Colina in the past."

Fernando nodded thoughtfully for several long moments. Then his face brightened. "Care to join me on a bit of a research expedition after this event is over? Purely for cultural reasons, of course."

Alex lifted an eyebrow. "I believe our plane is scheduled to leave at eight tomorrow morning."

Fernando shrugged. "We'll make it an early night, then. In bed no later than four."

Alex had heard that Fernando could be a bit dangerous when out on the prowl, and Alex not only had his own reputation but the reputation of Legado's new president to uphold. Still, it was difficult to avoid getting caught up in Fernando's enthusiasm.

"I've heard of a few places that might be ideal for your 'research.' And I'm sure they would love a visit from the future king of Léon."

"Excellent. One condition, though: you really need to stop calling me the future king of Léon. I already get all of the reminders I need about that from my father."

◊ ◊ ◊

Cap D'Antibes, South of France, 1965

Sandra wasn't sure why people took vacations. At least she wasn't sure why people from Legado took vacations. It couldn't be for the sunshine, as Legado's climate was exceedingly temperate and bright. It couldn't be for the beaches, since the shoreline in her homeland was pristine and plentiful. It couldn't be for the food, since Legado boasted some remarkable restaurants, and Sandra was sure that Legado home cooks were as fine as anyone anywhere. The Hotel du Cap in Cap D'Antibes was beautiful, and she appreciated her uncle's generosity in sending her to Europe, but the trip had been a long one and the experience, while entirely pleasant, hadn't been distinctive in any way. Maybe her expectations had simply been unrealistic. She'd been expecting the vacation to transform her somehow, to give her a new perspective on the world, and nothing of the sort had happened.

With only two nights left before she headed back home, Sandra wanted to try something different. Of course, her uncle had insisted on her being chaperoned, and her aunt's cousin Luciana had been by her side everywhere. Since Luciana was a simple woman, that meant early dinners and early bedtimes. Tonight, though, Sandra had pleaded that they go to the hotel lounge afterward to listen to music — several

English pop bands were playing under the banner "Britain Invades France" – and have a drink or two. As Sandra anticipated, Luciana was snoring in her chair within twenty minutes, leaving Sandra free to roam through the lounge.

A group of boys in Beatle haircuts were playing Herman's Hermits' "Mrs. Brown You've Got a Lovely Daughter" on the stage as Sandra moved up from the back of the room. A number of men tried to catch her eye, but she ignored them as a matter of course. From the time she'd entered her teens, Sandra had had reliable instincts about men; she could spot the ones that wanted to take advantage of her easily, and she'd quickly come to understand that the way a man regarded her accurately predicted whether or not he was going to let her down or even be a threat to her at some point. So far, the French men in this room did not impress her, and the other Europeans were underwhelming as well.

She took a quick glance back to see if Luciana was still sleeping. Indeed, she was. Sandra knew from the experience of the last two weeks exactly what Luciana looked like when she was snoring. And how she sounded. Sandra was a little surprised she couldn't hear the sound of her chaperone's foghorn over the band.

"Please tell me you don't need to leave," said someone in French.

The voice behind her startled Sandra. She turned to encounter a man perhaps a few years older than she and easily six inches taller. A quick glance showed that he was solidly built and well-groomed and that he had lovely eyes. A slightly deeper glance into those eyes showed that he had none of the traits that she'd found so easy to dismiss in the other men in the room. These were eyes of surprising depth, actually.

"Leave?"

The man gestured with his head toward the back of the room. "You'd turned toward the exit. I was hoping this didn't mean that you were leaving."

Even with the music playing loudly — another Herman's Hermits song, "Can't You Hear My Heartbeat" — Sandra was taken with the timbre of the man's voice. It was resonant, like a fine reed instrument. While he wasn't speaking particularly loudly, his voice commanded the space; Sandra had the feeling he knew how to get people to pay attention to him.

"No, I was just checking on something," she said in broken French. She'd had little reason to learn the language at home, and the quick studying she'd done before this trip had left her with a limited vocabulary, though she could understand better than she could speak.

"Then I can breathe easier," he said. "Might I interest you in a drink?"

Sandra offered him a tiny smile. "Yes. Yes, I think I'd like that."

They walked over to a corner table that was surprisingly open in the crowded lounge and ordered: Courvoisier for him, a Curacao Cocktail for her. It was only then that they exchanged names. His was Cayetano.

"You're not local," he said when their drinks arrived.

"No, I'm from Legado."

His eyes widened. "South America. That's quite some distance." Sandra noticed that the man had switched seamlessly from French to Spanish, her native language. "What brings you here?"

Sandra was relieved to switch to Spanish as well. "My uncle sent me on a European trip as a college graduation present. He thought it would be good for me to get away for a while. He thinks I'm trying too hard to be a career woman, and he thinks I should take some more time for myself to recalibrate my priorities."

Cayetano nodded slowly. "A career woman. What sort of career?"

"I'm fascinated with the stock market. I studied business and finance in college."

Sandra knew she was taking a chance bringing up the subject. She'd found few men who could appreciate the idea of a woman being interested in "men's things" such as money. Certainly, her uncle didn't appreciate it.

"Really," Cayetano said. "I have quite a great deal of interest in economics myself."

Sandra smiled more broadly now. "Then this will easily be the most interesting conversation I've had since I landed on this continent."

They spent the next several minutes discussing economic theory: how much of a threat rising inflation was to Legado's future, how realistic it was for both of their nations to stay on the gold standard, what the rise in socialism portended for capitalism. Sandra found that Cayetano had a keen mind. He also wasn't speaking with her as though she were a precocious child. One of the things she found frustrating about most of the people, even professors, she tried to engage in such conversation was that they seemed amused by her observations. It was as though they found it quaint that someone destined for a life as a homemaker could entertain such thoughts. Cayetano, on the other hand, took up the conversation with gusto, challenging her, debating her, and conceding a well-made point.

Their conversation did eventually move away from economics and toward more personal matters. Sandra learned that Cayetano was twenty-six, five years older than she, that he'd never been involved in a serious romance, and that his relationship with his family was complicated.

"They want me to be something I'm not sure I'll ever be," he said as he started his second Courvoisier. "They have this vision for me and," he laughed mirthlessly, "I'm not sure it can ever come true."

Sandra leaned toward him. "Do you want it to come true?"

"I do. Very much, actually. But so much is out of my control, and I feel that I should be preparing for reality as opposed to the fantasy they have in mind." He paused and pondered his drink for several seconds. "To tell you the truth, I'm sort of running away from my parents at the moment. I came to Cap D'Antibes to . . . escape."

Sandra found herself placing her hand on his, even though some might interpret that to be a brazen move. "I know exactly what you mean about the need to escape one's family. My father disappeared on us when I was still an adolescent. The rest of us moved in with my uncle. He takes good care of us, but he has conditions. Chief among his conditions for me is that I marry well. He fears that I'm bordering on spinsterhood."

Cayetano cocked an eyebrow. "How old did you say you were?"

"I turned twenty-one last month."

"Well, I see his point. You're ancient." Cayetano grinned at her to make it clear that he was joking.

"I wish I could find as much humor in this as you do."

He squeezed her hand. "I'm kidding with you, but I'm not taking what you're saying lightly. It's the sixties. Even in Legado, I assume. Your uncle needs to realize that the world is changing."

Sandra shook her head. "His world has been the same for generations. Tradition is everything to him."

"Then you need to step out."

"Easier said than done. He is becoming one of Legado's top politicians and could easily be president one day. He's now the ambassador to Italy and a very close advisor to our current president."

"Perhaps stepping out would be difficult." A sly grin rose on Cayetano's face. "But it would be very easy for you to step out onto the dance floor with me right now."

Sandra had largely forgotten that they were in a lounge and that there was music playing. As Cayetano rose and beckoned her to join him, though, she could hear the plaintive notes of The Righteous Brothers' "Unchained Melody."

The song was a challenge for the lead singer of the band at the lounge, but that made no difference to Sandra as she walked with Cayetano onto the dance floor and slipped into his arms. For the next thirty seconds or so, the music enveloped them, and Sandra warmed to Cayetano's closeness.

"I half-expected you to want to lead," he said, grinning at her.

"I would have taken over if you didn't know what you were doing, but you seem to be perfectly competent."

He chuckled and drew her closer, and they didn't speak for the remainder of the song. By the end of it, Sandra had laid her head on Cayetano's chest, swearing she could hear his heartbeat even with all of the sound around her.

After the song finished, the band switched tempos to The Beach Boys' "California Girls." For an instant, Sandra wondered at the fact that these "British Invasion" bands had started playing American pop songs, but that hardly mattered to her at the moment. Now that their dance had ended, Sandra took a step back toward their table, but Cayetano coaxed her into staying for the faster dance, getting a chuckle out of her when he switched the lyrics of the chorus to, "I wish they all could be Legado girls." For someone who'd exhibited such intellect earlier, he seemed especially proud of this extremely tiny display of wit.

The band took a break after that, and Sandra agreed to one more drink.

"I have some bad news," he said as they sat. "I need to leave for home in two days."

Sandra wrinkled her nose. "Me too. And I have worse news. I'm not alone here. My uncle sent me with a chaperone."

Cayetano rolled his eyes. "How did you get away tonight?"

"I didn't get away entirely. She's in the back of the lounge sleeping."

Cayetano leaned closer. "Did you drug her," he said mischievously.

Sandra grinned back at him. "No, but that's an option to consider in the future."

Cayetano reached out for her hand. "A walk outside?"

"I'd like that."

Without waiting for their drinks, and with Cayetano making a signing gesture to one of the waiters, they made their way out of the lounge. That was when Sandra noticed Luciana, still snoring and slumped further down in her chair. Sandra knew she couldn't leave Luciana like this. The woman would eventually awaken, and when she did, she would panic over not being able to find Sandra. And Sandra's uncle would be furious if he found out that Sandra had ditched her chaperone.

She explained the situation to Cayetano as they stood in front of the sleeping woman.

"Are you sure she won't simply keep snoring through our walk?" he said.

"She might. But she might not." Sandra looked down at the woman, wishing for some kind of sign. "I can't take that chance."

Cayetano's eyes dropped. "Then this is goodbye until tomorrow."

Sandra was surprised by how mournful he sounded and by how completely this echoed her feelings. "I guess it is."

He brightened. "Meet me by the pool in the morning." He gestured toward Luciana. "Bring her, if you must."

"I'll figure out something."

"Until tomorrow, then."

With that, he took her hand, kissed it softly, and walked away. Sandra watched him turn the corner and then rustled Luciana awake.

Perhaps this was why people went on vacations.

Chapter 2
New York, February

Alex always girded himself for an onslaught when he opened his email in the morning. It didn't happen often, as most of his Asian and European correspondence was collegial and procedural, but every now and then he needed to jump into crisis mode within minutes of awakening. The curious thing about these crises was that they had once energized him, left him feeling electrified for the day the way a good workout would. However, since he'd started getting Allie ready for school in the morning, he found that he didn't like being overly amped while he made her breakfast. If he'd had to take too many actions first thing in the day now, he felt as though he was short-changing his daughter because he wasn't truly with her during their mornings together. There was a time when he would have scoffed at any corporate leader who felt as though he could bifurcate his time between on-the-job and in-the-home, but Alex had come to realize that he was decidedly more productive when the day transitioned from a confrontation-free start, to a pleasant breakfast, to a full day of top-level competition.

Regardless, Alex continued to gird himself for an onslaught as he walked from his bedroom to his home office, and today the preparation was warranted. His in-box included at least three dozen messages with some variation on the phrase "Ólgar rant." After reading a few of these, Alex switched to his news aggregator to access the source. There was Romeo Ólgar – a handsome man in a severe way, close to Alex's age – threatening to pull Léon out of the European Union, claiming the EU's open borders had turned Léon into a weaker trade partner and that his country was carrying an undue burden because of its neighbors' fiscal ills. Ólgar wasn't entirely wrong about this, though he was overstating the case in the signature way that had catapulted him into office. Léon's relatively steady economy was being forced to help prop up the weaker economies in much of the rest of Europe, though Alex had never seen any figures that indicated that the country's trade opportunities suffered from being part of the EU, and he doubted such figures existed.

Alex would have written off Ólgar's speechifying as simple posturing if not for what the prime minister said directly after:

> It is time for the Léon media to set aside their partisan allegiances in the service of our nation's greater good. Reporting inaccurately on our finances and on the practices of our neighbors is damaging to the security of our country. Therefore, I have informed my office that we will curtail access to our daily briefings to any news organization that continues to perpetuate myths about our interactions with the rest of Europe.

Alex reread the quote to make sure he'd comprehended it correctly, then watched the speech on YouTube to be certain that nothing had been taken out of context. Was Ólgar really talking about limiting the press in his country? Could he even do so unilaterally? Alex was relatively certain that the prime minister and the parliament had broad governing latitude, but the king had certain veto powers over both, and there were very clear restrictions on what the prime minister could do on his own. Still, Léon had a fairly recent history of power overreach — something that several of the messages in Alex's in-box alluded to — so one never took this sort of thing lightly.

There was a very good chance that Ólgar was just taking an extreme position in order to advance his agenda. That was a classic move from the vast majority of politicians: rile up your base, unnerve your opponents, and then come back with something that was still aggressive but seemed reasonable in comparison. On the other hand, if Ólgar was seriously considering exiting the EU, and if he were really going to go to war with the press in his country, that would be disastrous on any number of levels.

One of those levels was the interests of Alex's corporation. He'd done quite a bit of business with Léon over the years, and he had controlling stakes in three companies there now. A few years back, at the request of the king, he put a consortium together to buy the local flagship airline carrier to prevent a bankruptcy situation that would have hindered Léon's fortunes and might have even forced nationalization. Alex had allegiances with the country that ran all the way to the top, and he was currently exploring two new opportunities. If Léon's political climate became too stormy, though, he'd need to think twice about those opportunities, and he'd almost certainly need to re-budget his expectations in the other companies. He hated the idea of doing this, but he couldn't allow himself to respond to Ólgar's rhetoric emotionally, as some of his associates had. Alex would need to take the same reasoned approach to this turn of events that he took to all others.

At the same time, he felt for the nation's people, many of whom had to be rattled to hear the kinds of words they hadn't heard since the days of El General. He could only imagine the day King Alfonso and the crown prince were having. He didn't want to add himself to a call list for the king that was likely to grow exponentially as America awakened, but he had a feeling that the prince might appreciate hearing from a good friend — one with a famously even temperament. Unfortunately, the call to Fernando's cell went to voicemail.

"Hey, buddy. It sounds like Romeo isn't exactly spreading the love over there. I'm sure you're up to your ears offering everyone you've ever met assurances. If you want to take a break from all of that, give me a call. I don't need assurances. I just want to know how you're doing. Maybe I can even offer you assurances instead."

Alex went back to his email onslaught, responding in measured tones to the most overwrought. There was no question that he was going to be distracted at breakfast this morning. He'd have to find a way to make it up to his daughter. Maybe tonight after dinner, they could go out for ice cream.

◊ ◊ ◊

Colina, 1992

Prince Fernando had an interesting suite of expressions. The one he was wearing just now was an ideal example: he somehow managed to look taciturn and carefree at the same time. Alex had found himself watching the man carefully as they moved from the bar with the nearly naked dancers to the bar with the raging thrash metal band to the bar with throbbing house music and considerably more throbbing in the VIP room. Fernando drank and talked up women, and drank and made "royal proclamations," and drank and challenged strangers to "arm wrestle with a prince." He was a genial drunk, never once offending anyone in the room. But a wave of darkness would shadow his face with regularity. The first several times Alex saw it, he expected an eruption of some sort from Fernando. After a while, though, Alex began to wonder if Fernando could even feel the emotions he was displaying.

"Alejandro Soberano," Fernando said, rising unsteadily from where they were sitting in a semi-private lounge, "you really know your Legado nightlife."

"I really don't. As I said, I never went out much when I lived in this country, and I haven't lived in this country in a long time."

"Then you're a natural. You have a deep innate talent for identifying places where we can drink Champagne and gawk at gorgeous women."

"I'll be sure to add that the next time I update my resume."

"Excellent idea. I'd hire you in a second. So, tell me more about what it is you do, Alejandro Soberano."

Alex thought it was funny how Fernando kept referring to him by his first and last name. He'd suggested that "Alex" would do the first several times and now just accepted that Fernando preferred it for reasons he was keeping to himself. "I work on mergers and acquisitions for a Wall Street bank. I headed up a project by myself for the first time a couple of weeks ago. It was an amazing experience. As good as the best sex I've ever had."

"Nothing is as good as the best sex I've ever had."

Alex chuckled. "Yes, well you're royalty. I've heard that royal sex is on an entirely different level from sex for us mere mortals."

Fernando seemed to absent his body for a few moments and then said dreamily, "Yes, royal sex is very exciting." After that, he offered a little laugh and then locked eyes with Alex. "But that's not what we were talking about. Mergers and acquisitions. You like doing this sort of thing, obviously."

"Either that, or I don't like sex. But yes, I like it quite a bit. I'm doing it for other people right now, but that is definitely not my long-term plan. I want to have my own corporation up and running by the time I'm thirty-five."

Fernando's expression showed a hint of surprise. "You said 'corporation,' not 'company.'"

"Yes, a corporation, as in a conglomeration of companies. I think I have a unique talent for making the right kinds of bets, and I intend to put that to maximum use."

Alex didn't mention that part of his "unique talent" was the ability to read at great depth the electromagnetic auras of the people with whom he did business. When you knew how much you could trust a company's executive management and when you could read how committed they were to their efforts, the company's prospects came alive in ways that could never be expressed on a balance sheet. Alex knew this gave him a tremendous advantage over his competition, and he pressed that advantage at every opportunity.

"I admire your ambition," Fernando said. "I don't have any ambition myself, but I can appreciate it when I see it."

"The future king of Léon doesn't have any ambition?"

"It turns out that none is required as long as the role stays in the future."

"But surely you've been training for that very future for years."

"My father is still a young man, and we haven't had a king assassinated in centuries. I'm not particularly worried about ascending any time soon. I mean, there's all of that princely twaddle I'm supposed to be handling, but I suppose I have a unique talent as well. Mine is for dodging my royal duties whenever possible."

Alex found this sort of talk exotic. Having graduated from the Massachusetts Institute of Technology and Harvard, two of the top universities in the world, and working in an ultra-competitive profession, he wasn't sure that he'd crossed paths with many unambitious people. Yet sitting across from him was someone who lived in a palace and seemed unmotivated to do anything other than order another bottle of wine.

"No hobbies?" Alex said.

Fernando gestured around the room. "Well, this is a hobby."

"I suppose it is in some way."

Fernando's expression shifted again, both less taciturn and less carefree. "You don't think much of me, do you?"

"No, that isn't true at all. For one thing, I find you to be extremely entertaining. I guess I'm just having some trouble understanding what it is like to live a life without passions."

Fernando leaned forward with a vividness in his eyes that Alex hadn't seen for at least two bottles. "I didn't say that I had no passions."

"Yes, I know, sleeping with twins."

"No, not that. Well, that, too. But I care quite a great deal about education, if you want to know the truth. I actually studied with Bruner. I can quote Piaget's writings verbatim. Did you know that Léon's educational system lags far behind most of the rest of Europe? I have a plan for that. I think you might even call it a passion."

The shift in tone startled Alex for a moment. Seeing Fernando talk about education was like watching one of those science fiction movies where an alien takes over a host body to deliver a message.

"That's wonderful," he said. "And it's so great that you have a plan for improving your country and you're in a position to put that plan in place."

Fernando's eyes dropped. "Ah. There's the problem."

"What do you mean?"

"My father has made it very clear that implementing this plan is outside of the range of my responsibilities and that the palace leaves education to the prime minister's government."

"He's the king; couldn't he just issue an edict?"

"You're aware that it's 1992, aren't you? Kings don't really do edicts anymore."

"I know, but he still wields considerable influence. And this is something that his son clearly cares about very deeply."

"He does wield considerable influence. On everyone. Including me. And what he has made clear is that the palace's role in governing our country is focused on the economy. Otherwise, ceremonial matters aside, the prime minister and his cabinet are in charge. The minister of education has decidedly different viewpoints from mine and has expressed no interest in an exchange of ideas."

Alex couldn't imagine what that would be like. To care deeply about something and be actively held back from doing it must be dreadful. That seemed to explain the complicated nature of Fernando's expressions: some part of his mind was always processing this, even when he was partying (which seemed to be most of the time).

"That must really suck for you," Alex said.

Fernando held his gaze for a moment. Then his eyes brightened and he gestured for a waiter. "The truth is that reforming education would be something akin to real work. What's the point of being a prince if you have to do real work?" He threw a gaze toward the corner of the room to his left. "I'm sure you've noticed that those women keep staring over here. I think it's time we ask them to dance."

◊ ◊ ◊

Anhelo

The travel party the next morning was almost comically small considering the size of Fernando's private plane: just Alex, Fernando, Legado's Minister of Foreign Affairs, Fernando's doctor (who traveled with him everywhere as required by the government of Léon), and a couple of bodyguards. The scale of the reception when the plane landed, however, was truly outsized. As Alex got off the plane, he was stunned to see the tarmac filled with a full military band, a panel of dignitaries, and what was easily five hundred locals who'd come to get a glimpse of the pop star prince.

The biggest surprise was when the band started playing as soon as Alex moved to the top of the stairs while Fernando was still on the plane. Alex continued down the stairs, glancing behind him to see if the prince had started his descent and still not seeing him. Things got even more baffling when the mayor of Anhelo stepped forward to shake Alex's hand. Was this because President Benigno was his cousin? That was difficult to believe, but Benigno was very popular. And Alex had to admit he enjoyed the attention.

At that moment, Fernando appeared at the door of the plane and waved to the crowd. The mayor threw a hand up to his face, glanced quickly at Alex and then again at the plane, and then stepped forward to greet the prince as he descended. It was at that point that Alex realized that the contingent from Anhelo had messed up. However, by then, everyone else in the line was greeting him as if he was the prince without realizing that the real prince was behind. They saw a man in his late twenties get off the plane and just assumed that man was the prince. Clearly, they didn't pay as much attention to the tabloids as Alex did (and even he hadn't recognized Fernando instantly when they first met). The Minister of Foreign Affairs scowled at him — as though Alex had somehow done something to draw this attention to himself — and gestured with her head toward a waiting limousine. Alex furrowed his brow at the minister, then grinned sheepishly at the people around him and headed to the car.

Fernando joined him a few minutes later. "So, how did you enjoy your minute as royalty?" he said.

"By the time I realized what was going on, it was over."

Fernando laughed. "Maybe I should have stayed on the plane. I could have sent you to cut the ribbon by yourself."

"They would have figured it out eventually, right?"

"Maybe. Maybe not. Perhaps they would have said to themselves, 'he is very handsome, but not as devilishly handsome as I'd always heard,' but they might have let it pass." He sat with this for a moment. "Now that I think about it, it's a good thing I got off the plane. I can't have people in Anhelo telling others that Prince Fernando is only very handsome."

The limo started moving at that point. There was a military convoy ahead of them and the band playing boisterously behind them.

Alex grinned at Fernando. "Yes, probably best all around."

Fernando chuckled. "Although, maybe we could switch places from time to time. After all, anybody can do what I do."

◊ ◊ ◊

Cap D'Antibes, 1965

Sandra considered a number of options for getting rid of Luciana. In spite of Cayetano's presumably playful suggestion, she never seriously considered drugging her chaperone. She did, however, consider bribing the hotel staff to detain the woman in some way, going to the bathroom during breakfast and sneaking from there to the pool, and an elaborate plot that involved a speedboat and two village urchins. In the end, Sandra took the boldest chance of all: she told Luciana the truth.

"A man? But when?" the woman said, her face wracked with confusion.

"Last night. While you were sleeping. You were very tired, and I didn't want to disturb you, so I wandered through the lounge a bit."

This seemed to baffle Luciana more, but then her eyes refocused. "Is he handsome?"

"Very handsome. With intelligent, kind eyes."

"And his lips?"

The question surprised Sandra, but she recovered quickly. "They haven't touched mine, if that's what you're asking."

Luciana smiled. "That was what I was asking. I'm glad they haven't touched yours − at least not yet. It means he isn't too forward."

Sandra recalled how it felt when Cayetano kissed her hand before they parted last night. She definitely wanted his lips elsewhere and would have gladly allowed it, but that wasn't something she needed to share with her chaperone. "He's a real gentleman, Luciana."

"That's good to know."

"And he wants us to spend the day together by the pool."

Luciana arched her eyebrows. "Without me, I assume."

"Preferably. No offense."

Luciana wrapped an arm around Sandra's shoulders. "There's no need to worry about offending me. I was twenty-one once. I know what it is like to find a man impossible to ignore."

To the best of Sandra's knowledge, Luciana had never had a man in her life, so this comment made her curious. That was a conversation for another day, however.

"So, you'll let me go?"

"Go. Be with your handsome man." Luciana held up a hand. "You know to protect your virtue, yes?"

"Of course, Luciana. I'm not the first flower of the spring. I know how to keep men under control."

"Yes, I've heard that about you. I sometimes feel sorry for the men. Enjoy your day. I will catch up on my reading."

Sandra was in her bathing suit and out the door only a few minutes later. She was poolside looking for Cayetano another few minutes after that. She didn't find him right away, and she worried that Cayetano's intentions hadn't been as pure as he'd suggested last night. Maybe he decided to go back to the lounge after they parted and he found a different woman with whom he would spend his last few days in France. One without a chaperone.

But then she saw him under a large red umbrella flanked by two men slightly older and slightly bigger than he was. Cayetano's eyes were closed, and he seemed intent on taking in the beautiful weather, though the other two men seemed satisfied to be watching the bathers around them. As Sandra approached the umbrella, one of the men stood, which caused Cayetano to open his eyes.

"You've come," he said. He rose from his chair and then asked the two men with him to excuse them, gesturing for Sandra to sit in the space one of Cayetano's friends had just vacated. "Is your chaperone watching from the bushes?"

"She might be, but I think she's decided to stay in our room. It turns out that she's a romantic."

"I could tell, even when she was snoring, that she had love in her soul."

Sandra settled back in her chair and tilted her face toward the sun. Cayetano leaned back at the same time and, as he did, he reached for Sandra's hand. They held hands in silence for several minutes, Sandra bathing in the warmth generated by the heat source above her and the one next to her.

"I think my mother might be a romantic," Cayetano said, his voice parting the layers of sound and sensation Sandra had settled into.

"You're not sure?"

"Well, how is anyone ever sure about that sort of thing?"

"Funny you would say that. I think it's a rather easy condition to diagnose."

"Hmm. Maybe I've spent too much time around my father."

"Not a romantic, I'm guessing."

"Whatever the polar opposite is. My father has been very explicit about his distaste for all things related to emotions."

"And yet your mother remains a romantic."

"She's guarded about it. Hence the difficulty in *diagnosing* her. But yes, I think she is. Every now and then throughout my life, she's spoken to me about the miracle that is love. I'm not sure how she knows about these things since, as you can imagine, my parents' marriage is not a loving one and there's no indication that it ever was."

Sandra was finding it fascinating that Cayetano would talk about this sort of thing with her in only their second conversation. Was he this candid with every woman he met?

Eventually, they spent some time swimming and then, after lunch, some more time on a sailboat that Cayetano had chartered for them. Their conversation didn't return to his parents' marriage, but they spoke lustily about finance and then somewhat more carefully about what they were doing with their lives. Cayetano made it clear that he'd been destined to go into the family business from the time he was born, another decision his father seemed to have made for him, though there also was some impediment that was making his role in the family business more elusive than Cayetano wanted. Every time Cayetano mentioned his father, Sandra found her ire building. One's fate shouldn't be determined by others, a point that she'd tried to impress upon her uncle on numerous occasions.

"What if you simply revolted?" she said as they watched the sun go down from one of the resort's cabanas.

"Revolted?"

"Yes. What if you just told your father that you weren't interested in being a part of his business any longer, that you wanted to set your own course."

Cayetano studied Sandra carefully for several seconds. "I think I might have misled you. I'm very interested in being part of my father's business. I find his work fascinating and what I do for him to be fulfilling. I just don't want to be my father."

Sandra took Cayetano's hand. "You will never be your father."

Cayetano smiled. "You know this for a fact."

Sandra knew he was teasing her, but she pushed forward. "I do. We've been together for less than twenty-four hours, but if I am certain about anything, I am certain that you could never be the person you describe your father to be."

Cayetano looked off in the distance for a moment before coming back to her. "Somehow hearing you say that makes me want it to be true."

Dinner was served to them at the cabana, after which Cayetano suggested that they return to the lounge. Sandra thought about the music the bands had been playing last night and knew that she wasn't in the mood for the British Invasion or even the American variation on it. She suggested the piano bar instead, and they sat there for as long as they could, sipping cocktails, slow-dancing to a few numbers. Eventually, though, the day — a day that had started more than a dozen hours earlier — had to come to an end. Sandra was certain that she had taken advantage of Luciana's good graces, and they had to leave for the airport early in the morning.

"I so wish you weren't leaving tomorrow," Cayetano said when he walked Sandra back to her room.

Sandra looked down at her hands. "Why couldn't we have met a week ago?"

Cayetano reached for her chin and tilted it upward. And then he was kissing her, the kind of kiss that declared that romance mattered to him and that this day had been to him what it had been to her.

"We will see each other again," he said.

"I hope so," Sandra said, though she wasn't sure how it would be possible.

Then he kissed her one more time, this kiss even more tender than the last, before taking a step back, touching her face, and turning to leave.

Sandra watched him until he was no longer visible and then she stayed outside a few more seconds before going into her room.

Chapter 3
New York, February

Alex's personal cell phone rarely rang while he was at work. He kept it on his desk primarily in case Allie or Angélica needed him, and they knew they should only use it under extreme circumstances. Alex once told his daughter that she shouldn't call him at work unless she were bleeding and then, seeing the hurt expression on her face, quickly amended it to, "Or if you just want to talk; that would be fine, too." He couldn't recall a single time when she'd done so, and he knew that he'd probably stung her with the comment more than he'd ever intended. Very few other people had his number: his mother, his sister, his brother, and a small handful of friends. Therefore, it always surprised him when he heard the ringtone: a rock version of the Legado national anthem that a guitarist friend had custom recorded for him. Hearing it now instantly pulled him out of the budget report he'd been reviewing.

A quick glance at the phone's screen identified the caller as "IV," Alex's shorthand for King Alfonso IV of Léon.

"Your Majesty."

The king had suggested to Alex several times that Alex didn't need to address him so formally, but Alex persisted. He enjoyed offering that level of respect to someone when he felt the person had earned it. And even though IV was king via birthright, he'd done more than enough to earn Alex's respect over the years.

"Alex, I hope I'm not disturbing you."

"Not possible in your case, sir."

"You're very kind. I suppose you've been keeping up with our news."

"It would be difficult to avoid. I think it is safe to say that the name of the prime minister of Léon has appeared in more of my email correspondence than all other European leaders combined."

Alex heard the king sigh. "I believe this puts the lie to that phrase that Americans like to say. How does it go: 'There's no such thing as bad publicity.'"

"Indeed. How are you holding up? I've spoken to Fernando a few times about Ólgar, but you and I haven't had the chance."

"I'm holding up fine. What choice do I have? I can certainly say that I've never had to deal with someone like Romeo Ólgar before during my years on the throne."

Alex imagined that this might actually be true. "Isn't it possible for you to insist that he dial things back? He reports to you, doesn't he?"

The king chuckled sadly. "The government of Léon is not a business organization, Alex. While the prime minister technically serves at my pleasure, our constitution long ago eliminated the power of the king to remove an elected official. I think Ólgar is very much aware that he 'reports' to no one."

Alex of course knew this. One didn't make significant investments in a country's businesses without understanding how that country operated. However, he also knew that, unlike in several countries, the king still had meaningful influence in Léon. If King Alfonso was saying that he couldn't extend this influence to Ólgar, this meant that he'd already tried.

"I'm very sorry to hear this, sir."

"I appreciate that. I've spent many hours — I've had extra ones lately, because I haven't been sleeping — trying to think of ways to offset the effect the prime minister is having on the country and all of Europe. I think the only answer is for the royal family to have a much bigger presence than it normally has."

"That makes perfect sense."

"There's only one complication: there's only so much of this I can do on my own."

This was the king's diplomatic way of saying that his son — and one of Alex's closest friends — wasn't up to the task of helping. Alex loved Fernando like a brother, but he was well aware of how little the prince resembled a true leader. Even at fifty, Fernando was much more likely to be in the news for a public display at a nightclub than for any work he was doing on behalf of the people of his nation.

"What can I do to help?" Alex said.

"Well, you've already helped simply by asking that question. The truth is that I'm not at all certain about what approach to take or what would be effective. All I know at this point is that we need to do something to show that Léon isn't doing anything that would signal a shift to the days of my predecessor. People on my staff have begun to refer to the prime minister as *General* Ólgar. You have no idea how chilling that is to me."

"I think I might have some idea."

"Yes, I suppose you would. I wanted to let you know that I'm convening a meeting with the best and the brightest, both inside Léon and out. You're the first person I called."

"I'm flattered."

"I need some of what you've brought to the business world, Alex. I'm especially intrigued by what you brought to social media with your Vidente platform. Something tells me there's an answer there. Is there any chance I can get you to fly here next week?"

Alex didn't need to look at his calendar to know how much was going on next week. His staff had been sending him preparatory memos about it for the past month. It was easily the most important week of the quarter. Possibly the year.

"I'll clear my schedule."

"You're a godsend, son."

◊ ◊ ◊

Castile, Léon, 1997

Even for someone who had heads of state in his family and who'd had an intimate relationship with a world-renowned diplomat, meeting a king was a big deal. This was especially true because the king was the head of the nation that had provided Legado with so much of its culture. And because the son of that king had become one of Alex's closest companions.

Alex and Fernando had developed an active relationship since they first met during the inauguration five years earlier. They spoke on the phone at least once a week, they'd gone clubbing during both of Fernando's visits to North America, and Fernando had met Alex when Alex went to London for a conference, leading to a night on the town that Alex could only hazily remember. Alex had neither the desire nor the stamina to keep up with Fernando's lifestyle on an ongoing basis, but he enjoyed their forays in short bursts, and he reveled in his ability to help Fernando avoid the paparazzi. Their time together pulled Alex out of himself, which was something he increasingly desired.

"My dad wants to meet you," Fernando had said during a call about a month earlier.

"Why would your father want to meet me?"

"Because I told him you're a genius, and he likes meeting geniuses."

"No pressure there."

"I thought you were impervious to pressure."

Alex shook his head, even though he knew his friend couldn't see him. "*Business* pressure. This is different."

"It'll be great. And I'll get to show you around the palace. You can stay in the Equine Room. Men have been known to become supernaturally virile after sleeping in the Equine Room."

"No doubt you've slept there many nights yourself."

"Don't you know it!"

And so, they'd arranged it, leading to the current antici-patory moment. Alex really had no reason not to meet King Alfonso. He'd admired what the man had been able to do for Léon after the demise of El General, and a visit with a royal family certainly qualified as a good use of his vacation time. Besides, the man had asked to meet him. Didn't that make this something of a command performance? Still, Alex felt surprisingly jittery as he waited in the library for the king's arrival.

"Rise up for your liege."

It took Alex a second to realize that the booming voice was Fernando's, by which point he was already standing, something he'd done entirely on instinct.

Fernando strode into the room grinning. "Oh, sit down. Where do you think you are?"

"I was planning to show your father his due respect."

"Well, in that case, you should be kneeling with your head bowed."

At that point, the king entered the room. King Alfonso IV was in his late fifties, trim, and showing just a hint of crow's feet at his eyes. Though Alex was approximately the same height as the king, the man's sense of presence made him seem taller. Alex vowed to understand how that worked.

"Don't listen to my son," the king said, extending his hand. "As you've probably learned by now, he likes to exag-gerate."

Alex shook the king's hand, thankful that he himself had been blessed with a firm grip. "I have no idea what you're talking about, Your Majesty."

"Ah, you are a good friend, aren't you?"

They sat, and there was an immediate frenzy of activi-ty in the room, as various staff members brought coffee and pastries, made other arrangements at the table, and confirmed that the king was comfortable. Alex found this sort of thing fascinating. He'd attended meetings with some of the most powerful CEOs in the world and had never witnessed this level of care. For his part, the king seemed slightly uncomfortable with all of it.

"My son tells me you're planning to take over the financial world in the near future," the king said.

Alex smiled. "Well, 'take over' is a bit strong."

"From what he's told me, you have an unusually keen business sense."

Alex wasn't entirely sure how to play this conversation. Did he affect modesty in the presence of a man born to such a high station? Something told him that King Alfonso wouldn't appreciate that.

"I have been able to diagnose deals with a very high level of accuracy, Your Majesty."

"To what do you attribute your success?"

Alex wondered exactly how much he should share here. He'd acknowledged to very few people that his success had come in part from being able to read the electromagnetic fields around any potential business partner, and this definitely didn't seem the time to bring it up. "Paying careful attention, sir."

The king laughed. "That's it? Certainly, plenty of others pay attention when doing due diligence."

"I'm guessing that I do it differently from most. I believe it is important to calculate the true desires of top management."

"So, you think a company is more than its financial statements."

"Which is not to say that financial statements aren't important. But anyone can read a balance sheet. Reading the motives and intentions of a company's leaders is considerably tougher."

"I'll say. And you believe you can do this."

"As I mentioned, sir, I've had a decent amount of success with it."

Fernando reached for a pastry. "Alex plans on launching a corporation by the time he's thirty-five." It was the first time his friend had spoken since they sat down, and the prince immediately receded back to enjoy the cake he'd chosen.

"By thirty-five," the king said. He arched an eyebrow. "It's good to have a goal, I suppose."

Rather than trying to justify his ambitions, Alex took a sip of his coffee. The king held Alex's gaze for a bit longer and then did the same.

Several seconds passed before the king spoke again. "Entrepreneurialism among Léon citizens under thirty is lagging behind most of the rest of the developed world."

"I'm aware of that."

"Do you have any thoughts about why this might be?"

Alex took no time answering. "The government hasn't made it a cultural imperative. Socialism is too strong in Léon. The government provides all of the basic services, and this suppresses the ambition of entrepreneurs. You've essentially announced that innovation is not a priority."

The king tipped his head forward. "I would beg to differ."

"No offense, Your Majesty, but you might think you're prioritizing innovation and entrepreneurialism, but your social safety net, your tax structure, your grant offerings, and your banking system all say otherwise. A century-old furniture manufacturer is likely to find conditions considerably more favorable to him than someone with a new technology idea."

The king seemed to give this considerable thought. Then he nodded very slowly and took a long sip of his coffee. Alex wondered if he'd offended the man, but a quick glance at the king's aura suggested that he'd engaged him instead.

Alex continued. "My guess is that if you tracked the number of top Léon students over the past decade who have begun enterprises in the US or Singapore, you'd find that number to be rising."

"So, you're saying that we're telling our best young innovators that they should innovate elsewhere."

"I'm not saying that I know this definitively, sir, but I think a bit of research might bear this out. I know several people from Léon in New York and London who are doing very well. We keep track of that in the banking world."

The king sat back and put a finger to his temple. Alex felt flattered by how much thought the man seemed to be giving everything Alex was saying. He wondered if this was something the king did with everyone.

"How long are you planning to visit with us?" the king said.

"I'm here until Saturday."

"That's good. There are some people I'd like you to meet."

King Alfonso was gone about fifteen minutes later, but not before he and Alex had had a spirited conversation about an economy having an accommodating monetary policy. They would be having dinner with the rest of the family that night.

It dawned on Alex after the king left that Fernando's entire contribution to the conversation had been to eat three pastries. He looked a little wistful about it.

"Sorry, was that weird for you?" Alex said once the king was gone.

"No, it went about exactly the way I expected it to go. That's why I brought the two of you together."

"It's just that you didn't say anything, and I didn't know if that was because you were upset."

"Not upset; just out of my depth. Do I wish I could have a conversation like that with my father? Yes, I do. But not enough to actually learn about the things that truly matter to him. The reality is that a lot of the same things you were discussing would benefit from sweeping education reform, but that sort of talk never gets anywhere with my father. So, I serve as a spectator during conversations like these. At least I have you as my surrogate."

Alex smiled in response.

"Just to be clear, though," Fernando said with a grin, "I still get the inheritance."

"Understood."

◊ ◊ ◊

Milan, Italy, 1966

Sandra stood rigid as the seamstress fussed over the neckline of her dress. They'd been at this for nearly an hour now, and all Sandra wanted to do was sit down with a cappuccino and some cookies.

Sandra had heard from some of her friends that the days being fitted for their wedding dresses were among the most thrilling of their lives. And none of them had flown to Milan for the experience, because none of them had an uncle who'd been named ambassador to Italy and had used his influence to procure the finest wedding dress designer in this city of fashion. Yet it was difficult for Sandra to see the experience as anything more than a chore. Yes, the silk felt lush on her skin and, yes, the beading on the sleeves was intricate and elegant. And, yes, the dress being made for her was a one-of-a-kind, something she never anticipated she would ever have the means to wear.

If only she were wearing it for a more heart-fulfilling occasion.

The last year had been the most emotionally tumultuous of Sandra's life. She'd embarked on a career that offered glimpses of excitement but more often showed her the limitations of a woman participating in the pursuits of men. Often, her employers dismissed her ideas without any consideration, and the projects she received were consistently less challenging than those of the men who started at the same time she did. Even when she completed her work far ahead of the others, she only earned another desultory assignment.

Meanwhile, she'd come home from her magical last days in Europe and Cap D'Antibes filled with thoughts of Cayetano, the man who'd awakened romantic yearnings she didn't know she possessed. There was a letter from him waiting for her upon her return home, and they'd corresponded regularly in the time since. Cayetano promised they'd see each other again with a sincerity that filled Sandra with hope that he'd find a way. It was a hope she continued to cherish until the day her uncle called her into his study.

"I've found a good man for you," he said, packing a pipe with the stringent tobacco that smelled like pestilence when he burned it.

"Are you playing matchmaker now, Tio?"

His lip curled. "I'm not talking about introducing you to someone who might take you to dinner. I'm talking about your future husband."

Sandra found this conversation confusing at the start. Her uncle wasn't the kind of man who would have ever conjectured that he'd discovered her ideal mate. Like Cayetano's father, there was nothing about her uncle that was romantic. It wasn't until he explained further that Sandra understood what he was saying: as her guardian – even though she was technically an adult – her uncle had determined that she was getting past marriageable age and had taken it upon himself to arrange a union for her. The husband he had in mind came from a prestigious lineage, her uncle said; it was good for the family. Sandra soon came to learn that this prestige was the product of accomplishments that dated back more than a century and had been eroding ever since, but the name still carried some relevance in certain social circles. The family got invited to the right parties, not something that ever mattered terribly much to Sandra. However, she could see how it might matter to her uncle the ambassador.

Sandra had given so little thought to marriage that she wasn't sure whether to be devastated by her uncle's pronouncement or merely annoyed. The next week, when she met Sebastian, the other end of this transaction, and discovered that he was a man she would have dismissed instantly if she'd met him in a different setting, Sandra grew increasingly unsettled about the situation she'd been thrown into. But then the reality of the circumstances presented itself to her: she wasn't likely to find a husband who mattered to her in Legado, Sebastian was willing to let her continue to work — encouraged her, actually — and she'd likely had the only moment of ardor she was ever going to have while on a European vacation that was now in her past. And as she got to know Sebastian, she found him increasingly charming. He was a remarkably good dancer, and when they were on the dance floor, Sandra could feel something akin to chemistry between them, and that's when she noticed how good-looking he was. Life would not be unbearable with Sebastian; it might even be entertaining. And so, she attended the engagement parties with her most radiant smile, and she participated in the wedding preparations. And she allowed Milan's most celebrated designer to fit her for her dress.

The morning extended to the afternoon. Sandra finally got her cappuccino and cookies, but not until she was back in her hotel room, feeling as though she'd been laboring on a Joya de la Costa farm for a week. That night, she insisted on dining alone in the hotel's restaurant as she was alone in Milan since her uncle was in Rome at the embassy. She'd had enough of people circling around her and imagining how thrilled she must be to be preparing for such a lavish wedding and such a singular moment in her life.

She'd been given a lovely corner table, thankful that no one was questioning why she was eating alone. She'd settled back to peruse the menu while sipping a glass of Chianti when she heard the chair across from her pulled back. She looked up to see Cayetano smiling as though he'd just pulled off the cleverest magician's trick.

Sandra found herself momentarily flustered. Nothing about this trip had prepared her for this meeting. "I don't understand" was all she could think of to say.

"Do you mean your letter describing your visit to Milan wasn't an invitation to join you?"

Sandra had continued her correspondence with Cayetano, even after her betrothal, convincing herself that it was nothing more than a way to sustain a fantasy a little longer. In her last letter to him, she'd mentioned that she was coming to Italy and the reason why. She certainly hadn't intended it to be an invitation, but now she wondered if some part of her mind wished it to be true as she composed the note.

"But how did you find me? I didn't say where I was staying."

"It wasn't difficult to deduce. Appearances are obviously very important to your uncle and this is the finest hotel in Milan. That you would be eating here now — and by yourself — was purely conjecture on my part. Is it okay if I join you?"

Sandra got up from her seat and hugged him, holding him longer than might be considered appropriate in a public place with a man who was not her fiancé. She felt tears in her eyes and battled them back. Then she took a deep breath and returned to her seat.

"A bit of company might be nice," she said wryly.

"Well, we both need to eat."

For the next hour and a half, they talked the way old friends do, catching each other up on family, work, and local gossip. Cayetano was an entertaining dinner companion, capable of pivoting from incisive analysis of European markets to lampooning the latest British sex scandal without hesitation. While Sandra was abundantly aware of the fact that his presence here was a complication she hadn't anticipated, dinner passed effortlessly and was easily the most enjoyable time she'd spent since she landed in Italy.

At the end of the meal, Cayetano suggested that they skip coffee and instead walk to a café a few blocks away. Sandra welcomed the opportunity to extend their evening and thought the fresh air might be beneficial. As they left the restaurant, Sandra noticed two men following them from a respectable distance. Bodyguards. Of course, Cayetano would have bodyguards. He said that his father would never let him travel without them. What must it be like to have that kind of wealth? That kind of fiscal responsibility? That kind of predetermined future — right down to the pool from whom he could choose his bride, a pool that decidedly did not include a simple woman from Legado.

Sandra looped an arm around his as soon as they stepped outside. They'd only taken a few steps beyond the hotel's doors when she found the nerve to ask the question she'd been considering from the moment she saw him.

"What are you doing here, Cayetano?"

"I don't suppose you'd believe that I happened to be in the neighborhood."

"I wouldn't."

"No, of course you wouldn't." He tightened his arm on hers and looked outward. "I needed to make sure you were okay."

"But why wouldn't I be okay?"

Cayetano turned to look at her, and he captured her eyes. "It's me, Sandra. There's no need for pretending. Your letters have sounded unsettled."

Sandra looked away and urged their movements forward. "I've settled. This marriage will put me in a good place."

"A good place? But a person like you deserves a great love."

"Maybe great love is for other people."

Cayetano stopped and turned her toward him. "You don't really believe that, do you?"

She couldn't hold his gaze. "I will believe what I need to believe in order to get by."

Cayetano pulled her close to him at that point and said nothing for several long seconds. Then he kissed the top of her head and pulled back just enough to look at her.

"If my situation were any different, I would move heaven and earth to be that great love for you."

Sandra felt the tears returning to her eyes and again fought to keep them at bay. "I understand. Much as I don't want to. And I ask that you understand that I must do what I need to do."

Cayetano closed his eyes and then opened them again very slowly. "I do. And right now, there's something that I desperately need to do."

The passion in his kiss was unlike anything she experienced the last time they'd been together. It was as though he'd been storing all of his emotion for this one moment. Sandra found her defenses crumbling and her own passion rising to meet his. All through dinner, she'd been trying to convince herself that she could see this man and not get swept up in him. Now she realized she had been fooling herself. She could never be with Cayetano and not want him desperately.

"My hotel is a few blocks away," he said and, with no other words, they walked in that direction.

◊ ◊ ◊

Sandra awoke in the morning to Cayetano's kisses on her shoulder. She moved to him and he enfolded her in his arms. They kissed, and Sandra could feel her hunger rising again. In some distant part of her mind, she considered the possibility that what she was doing was wrong or even immoral, but she immediately quieted those thoughts. This was her moment, and she was going to live it.

Eventually, she glanced over at the clock. Her next fitting was a little more than an hour from now.

"I need to get back to the designer," she said.

"I know. How long are you staying?"

"Three more days, if nothing goes wrong."

"In that case, I hope things go terribly wrong and you need to stay for a month."

Sandra smiled at him. "Were that such a thing was possible."

He touched her face gently. "I want to be here every moment that you are here. No matter how long that is, it will never be enough."

"We will make it enough." She kissed him softly. "We need to."

Chapter 4
Léon, February

Alex had encountered his share of blustery person-
alities in his career. When one did most of one's
business with C-level professionals, one dealt with
a fair amount of bluster. And then, of course, there was his
ex-wife who, during their divorce negotiations, had turned
bluster into an art form. Still, he wasn't sure what to expect
from Romeo Ólgar. Alex had arrived in Léon the day before,
having answered King Alfonso's call for help, and today they
were meeting with the prime minister, ostensibly to discuss
expanding Alex's business interests in the country, but mostly for Alex to size up the man, so he could better counsel the
king on keeping Ólgar in check.

Predictably, the prime minister was fifteen minutes late,
clearly unconcerned that he was keeping the king − technically, his boss − waiting. Ólgar blew into the room with
his retinue, taking the end of the table on the other side and
settling into his chair noisily.

"Sorry to be late, Al," he said. "Never a dull moment, as
you can imagine."

Alex had never heard anyone refer to IV as "Al" before,
and he guessed that his good friend, who he would never call
by that name, didn't much care for it. To the king's credit,
though, "Al" betrayed no sign of irritation.

"Understood, Mr. Prime Minister. Allow me to introduce you to Alex Soberano."

Alex walked over to shake Ólgar's hand. As he did, he reset his vision to observe the aura around the man. Ólgar would believe that Alex was making eye contact with him, even though Alex was looking around him. It was a trick he'd perfected decades earlier. Alex had become so adept at this over the years that the entire thing would take no longer than a couple of seconds, and the prime minister would never know what happened.

Except in this case, Alex couldn't get a clear reading. This wasn't like the long period after Viviana died when he couldn't read personal acquaintances at all; he was getting a reading here, but it was an amorphous one. It was as though Ólgar's aura was executing some kind of evasive maneuver on him.

"Yes, Soberano," Ólgar said. "You're from Legado, right?"

"I was born there, yes. I've been living in the United States since college. I'm an American citizen now and I am also a Léon citizen, as your predecessor gave me an honorary passport due to my expanded business here. Today, I travel around Europe very proudly with my Léon passport."

"Right." He gestured Alex back to his seat. "Well, let's get to work and find out if you have anything to offer us so you can continue to be proud of that passport."

Anything to offer us? Alex thought. Alex had met with heads of state all over the world, and none had ever begun a meeting by saying something like that. What Alex and any corporate leader had to offer was revenue and jobs, commodities that usually prompted governments to express what *they* had to offer in terms of grants and tax advantages.

Alex took a quick glance over to IV, who offered him an arched eyebrow then turned to face Ólgar.

"Alex has significant stakes in three companies in Léon currently and controls our flagship airline carrier that he and the investment team he organized saved from bankruptcy. He has expressed an openness to expanding upon that."

Ólgar nodded stiffly. "Right. You know, of course, that my administration has been actively discussing lowering the percentage of foreign ownership we will allow in any company in Léon. It is critical that we do this to avoid any security risk."

Alex wasn't aware of this, and he quickly got the sense that this was news to the king as well. "I'm not interested in taking a majority position in any new company right now, so that shouldn't be a problem."

"I'm not talking about majority positions. I'm talking about something considerably less than that. *Considerably* less. There's far too much foreign influence on commerce within our nation. We might even be imposing tariffs on goods from several nations to protect our dying industries. That was part of my campaign platform."

Alex was beginning to wonder why Ólgar had agreed to have the meeting at all. Once again, he tried to read the prime minister's aura and again encountered the same disquieting amorphousness. He had no trouble reading the others in the room. What was the story with Ólgar's aura?

The meeting had begun inauspiciously, and it never improved over its half-hour duration. Alex was here under the pretext of expanding his holdings in Léon, but that wasn't a particular priority for him. If it had been, he would have left the conference room not only feeling discouraged about the possibilities but also wondering if he was going to be required to sell off some of the shares he already owned. This was going to require a serious conversation with the king. If Léon reduced its interest in foreign investment, the upshot might be a diminished role for the country in the international community. It made no sense for any number of reasons.

In many ways, this was consistent with many of Ólgar's other public positions, so it wasn't entirely a surprise; the man simply didn't seem to be putting his country ahead of his personal agenda. What was surprising was what Alex had seen — or rather not seen — in the prime minister's aura. He was going to need to do some serious exploration into this.

Once back at his rooms, Alex turned off his phones and took himself down into a deep meditative state. There, he reached out to Vidente, his late great-grandmother with whom he'd had regular spiritual contact since their dreamlike meeting on a cliff side at The Ashram in California a dozen years earlier. It was a meeting that understandably changed the course of Alex's life, focusing him more intently on personal relationships and on enterprises with greater import than some that had previously existed in his portfolio. It also left him with the most surprising familial companion he'd ever had, one he "visited" with regularly.

"There's a good deal of brown around you today, *tatara-nieto*. What is confusing you?" she said when they connected.

Alex always appreciated that there was no need for preface with Vidente. Yes, he would catch Vidente up on what was happening with Angélica and Allie, but they would take care of their pressing business first. "I saw something I've never seen before, *abuela*. Have you ever encountered an aura that refused to be read?"

Vidente was quiet for several seconds. "You're having trouble reading again? Have you been misbehaving?"

Vidente was making reference to the stretch of time after Viviana's death when he lost his ability to read auras in anything other than a business setting. Vidente helped him to find a way to get past this, but she never let him forget that his actions — specifically the way things had ended so badly with Viviana — had once left him diminished.

"No, not at all. I could read everyone else in the room. But one man — a very powerful man — was impossible to read. It wasn't as though there was nothing there, only that the colors kept eluding me."

"You tried going deeper?"

Vidente had taught Alex a method for "going beyond the colors" when a reading seemed inconclusive. That took the kind of time and concentration Alex didn't have in the conference room.

"I couldn't. But even if the conditions made it possible, I don't think it would have mattered. Going beyond the colors requires a color being there in the first place."

"And there was no color."

"It was bewildering. I could see the shape of the aura, but no color within the aura."

"I need to think about this."

"Please do. I went into this meeting concerned, and I came out considerably more concerned."

Alex knew that Vidente would attend to this from her own timeless space. Alex tried to wrap his mind around how her level of existence worked. He'd seen his great-grandmother, or at least her spectral form, but he didn't imagine her having a physical or temporal presence. Where and when was Vidente while they were speaking? When she said that she would think about Ólgar, was she doing so in the same time frame that he was, or was time an outmoded construct for her? Confounded as he was by his meeting with the prime minister, Alex found this additional line of thought more than he could maintain at the moment.

That night, Alex and the king met for a quiet dinner. At least it was as quiet as such an event could be when there was a half-dozen attendants hovering around them for the entire meal. The king's wife was away at a function of some sort for one of her philanthropies — Alex hadn't seen her on any of his last four visits to Léon — and Fernando wasn't getting back from his latest vacation until tomorrow. Considering the number of evening events the king always needed to fit into his schedule, Alex suggested they only have a quick drink so IV could enjoy a rare night off, but the king insisted on dinner.

"Our prime minister was at the top of his game today, wasn't he?" the king said as he sipped a sherry.

"He certainly came as advertised. How do you feel about his talk of isolationism?"

"The same way I feel about so much of his talk. Bewildered. Wondering which of us is the deluded one."

"Well, Your Majesty, if you're deluded, I'm experiencing the same affliction."

"That's why I asked you to come. I needed to make sure this wasn't about my growing out of touch. What were your other impressions?"

"I haven't been able to process all of them yet. Can I get back to you in the morning?"

Having decided not to do so at their first meeting decades earlier, Alex had subsequently never discussed his ability to read auras with the king, unsure that the man would be able to align their shared passion for business with Alex's long connection to the world of metaphysics and the practical applications his abilities had provided.

"Yes, of course," the king said. "Let's not talk anymore about Ólgar tonight. We could both use an evening's respite. Tell me how that remarkable daughter of yours is doing."

Alex settled back in his seat. "Ah, we've moved from the incredibly complex to the utterly simple. My daughter is the most perfect thing on the planet and no one is more aware of this than I am."

IV smiled warmly. "Surely your wife believes this as well."

"She does, but she allows the tiniest bit of pragmatism to creep into their relationship. I have no such room for this."

The king laughed, gesturing for one of the attendants to refill his glass. "I know exactly what you mean. That was me and Sabina."

The smile remained on the king's face as he seemed to get lost in thought, but his eyes clouded. Alex had never met Sabina, IV's middle child who died in a skiing accident two years before Alex met Fernando. To hear Fernando tell it, the king sequestered himself for months after Sabina died, even considering abdication because he wasn't sure he still had the will to rule. Fernando was quick to note that he was sure his father would do the same if he died, the only difference being that the grieving period would last hours instead.

"Fathers and daughters," IV said wistfully.

"They turn the strongest of us into weaklings."

"And happily so."

Alex grinned. "Yes, happily so."

Alex often wondered if he would have had a different relationship with a male child or even with just a second child. Angélica and he had considered growing their family back when Allie was younger, but it had never happened for a variety of reasons. Considering how he and the king seemed to be similarly in thrall to their daughters, Alex wondered if he would have had the kind of less-idyllic relationship IV had with his sons. Fernando's proclivity for man-child behavior was almost certainly specific to Fernando himself, but the king was considerably more distant from his youngest child whether Javier was in rehab or out. Alex had seen the king and Javier together on a couple of occasions and the pained expression the king wore during these visits spoke of a parental experience entirely foreign to Alex's understanding. The last he'd heard, Javier was once again under full-time care, attempting to break a dependency on opioids.

Alex examined the crystal goblet holding his Marques de Riscal Gran Reserva. "You know, Allie would love it here. She's quite fond of luxury. I think she secretly believes she's royalty."

The king laughed. "Well, I suppose that's what happens when one's parents treat one like a princess, no?"

"Yes, it might very well be all our fault."

"Why don't you have Angélica and Allie get on a plane to meet us? I haven't seen either of them in a couple of years. They could have the run of the palace while we were working together."

Alex laughed. "You have no idea what you'd be getting yourself into if you gave the two of them the run of the palace."

IV chuckled along. "Well, maybe just the north wing. I'm serious, Alex. It would be nice to have some youthful feminine energy around here."

Alex considered this. He didn't love pulling Allie out of school for any reason, because he felt that it was important that she always see school as a priority. Still, it was difficult to argue that it wasn't worth missing a week of classes to experience the inner workings of a major European palace. In addition, Angélica was currently writing a couple of long-form pieces that she could as easily write from the anteroom of their suite here as she could from her home office.

"Just so you're aware," Alex said, "Allie will tax the limits of your pastry chef's creative talents."

"I'm sure our pastry chef would welcome the challenge."

"Then I guess I'll call them."

"I'm glad to hear it. It's nice to make something productive out of a difficult day."

◊ ◊ ◊

St. Tropez, South of France, 1995

Alex had finally learned how to pace himself while out with Fernando. It was a matter of survival. While their body types were very similar (though Fernando was certainly a bit heavier), their metabolisms clearly weren't. On the first few of their weekends together, Alex had tried to match Fernando drink for drink, thankful that the prince always had a doctor in his traveling party. His memories of those excursions were Sunday mornings with a pillow over his head while his stomach insisted he book an extra couple of days at the hotel so he could take up residence in the bathroom. Alex had always considered himself a fast learner, but it took until the fourth party weekend with his friend, the prince, before he acknowledged that he was going to have to approach alcohol differently. Fernando didn't seem bothered that Alex was filling his Champagne glass less frequently than Fernando himself was. Maybe he just assumed that none of his companions could ever drink as much as he could and had been expecting this adjustment from Alex all along.

The VIP room in this particular St. Tropez nightclub was new to them, but it was a close cousin to every VIP room they'd visited before: throbbing music, throbbing patrons, and throbbing bravado. Alex supposed that professional sports locker rooms might be able to match the level of testosterone spewed all over a VIP room, but there was no other close competition. The place was thick with it. Fernando was very much in his element.

"I want some steak tartare," Fernando said as he started gesturing to a server. "Do you think they have it on the menu?"

Alex wasn't sure the club even had a menu. "I'm going to say no."

"But they'd get some for me, right?"

"Well, they do say they treat everyone like a king here, so they probably extend that treatment even to people who are only in line to be king."

"Yes, exactly!"

The server came over, and Fernando explained in great detail just the type of steak tartare he wanted delivered to their table. After his second bottle of Champagne, Fernando often grew hungry, which meant that Alex had witnessed the prince procuring everything from *gambas al ajillo* using only Calabrian chilies to *alfajores* made by a particular Argentinian baker who'd come to Europe to open a shop in Seville. By comparison, steak tartare, likely available from the restaurant next door, was a modest request, and he was sure that the club would do whatever was necessary to fulfill it.

"How is your father's small business initiative going," Alex said after the server left.

"How would I know?"

"It seems to me to be the sort of thing you could sink your teeth into. It's the right scale, it's all about teaching people new tools, and you could probably incorporate some ideas from your education plan."

Fernando smirked. "Might as well use them there, huh? Especially since I'm never going to be able to use them in *actual* education."

"That wasn't what I meant."

"I know. That would be reality, though, wouldn't it?"

"Maybe it could be a gateway."

"Like marijuana?"

"I was thinking of a different kind of gateway, but sure."

Fernando grinned and studied Alex, as though he were running through a list of possible actions from hugging him to slapping him across the side of the head. Then his expression darkened.

"It wouldn't be a gateway," he said. "It would be a sinkhole."

"Why do you say that?"

"Because it would give me an *engagement*. I'd wind up bogged down in this thing for the next eighteen to twenty-four months. Eighteen to twenty-four months doing something about which I don't care in the least. What's that going to do for me?"

Alex shrugged. "It would be a mission."

Fernando rolled his eyes. "A mission. You know, there are two types of people in the world: those who believe everyone should have a mission and those who realize that missions are a crutch."

With that, Fernando drained another glass of Champagne, as though this somehow underscored how little he needed crutches.

"You're coming up on your thirtieth birthday, Fernando. Aren't you concerned about the implications?"

"What implications? I'm rich, I travel regularly all over the globe, my face is in the papers all the time, and half the women in the world want to hook up with me. How many people do you know who have accomplished that much before their thirtieth birthday?"

Alex tilted his head toward his friend. "That's an interesting use of the word *accomplish*."

"You know what I'm saying."

"I'm not entirely sure that I do."

Fernando's brows furrowed. "Do you really want to get into this?"

"I think it might be a good thing if we did."

Fernando shifted in his chair, and Alex thought it was possible that they might actually engage, right here with the pulsating rhythms and the steak tartare in transit. Then Fernando's eyes diverted, and he smiled broadly.

"Speaking about getting into things, there's Claudia Svensen. Hey, Claudia!"

The supermodel/actress offered Fernando one of her electric smiles and made her way toward their table. This prompted Fernando to order two more bottles of Cristal.

Alex just shook his head and chuckled, though he wasn't terribly amused.

Later that night, Alex had to take Fernando out of Claudia's room as he had passed out on her while he was trying to do a line of coke on top of her crotch. She got scared and called Alex to come and rescue him, and Alex handled the whole incident without bothering the prince's doctor and without anyone ever knowing anything about it.

◊ ◊ ◊

Anhelo, Legado, 1966

Sandra ran for the bathroom the moment she awakened, thankful once again that she shared this space with no one else. "Just a nervous stomach," she'd said when her cousin had questioned her lack of appetite yesterday. "I so want all of the wedding plans to go smoothly." The lie went unnoticed. Every family had seen its share of nervous brides; it wouldn't be difficult for Sandra to convince others that she was the latest.

But Sandra knew her own mind. She knew that she wasn't fixated on the proper color transitions to the floral arrangements or whether the cellist in the string quartet would drown out the violins. She'd attended to the details studiously, and everything was likely to go as well as it needed to go and certainly far better than it mattered to her that they go.

More significantly, Sandra knew her own body. Her digestive system had been roiling for days, but the wedding that was happening this weekend had nothing to do with that. In fact, it couldn't have been further from the cause. Sandra knew the source of the nausea. Just as she knew that this nausea wasn't going to abate on Monday. From what she'd heard, women could contend with this sort of thing for a few months.

Now that she'd temporarily alleviated the problem, Sandra sat on the edge of her bathtub and rubbed her forehead. As had happened so often in the past month, her heart traveled back to her last few days in Milan. Other than the frustratingly long time she spent with the designer, she spent every minute of those days with Cayetano. On their second night together, he'd taken her to a tiny restaurant with only three tables where the owner had doted on them as though they were family. It was the only two hours they spent in public. For that matter, it was just about the only two hours they spent together when they weren't in bed. Sandra hadn't anticipated the hunger she would have for Cayetano because she'd never registered even the slightest version of this hunger for any man before. She wanted Cayetano's skin on hers, his whispers in her ears, his chest as a pillow, and she'd wanted it to the exclusion of everything else. The day they parted, Sandra grieved as though she'd just buried a close family member. But her body ached in a way that seemed as much physical as it was emotional. It was as though she was experiencing some level of withdrawal, like a drunk in the throes of the DTs.

That physical sensation had slowly faded over the past month. Now there was a new one. Sandra had never experienced this before, either, but she understood innately what was going on.

She hadn't given more than a few moments thought to how she was going to handle this. It wasn't as though there were terribly many options. Of course, Sebastian could never know. It wouldn't be difficult to deceive him; her future husband seemed to be oblivious to the ways of the female of the species. Keeping up the façade with the women in her family — and his — might be a bit more difficult, but if she were fortunate, she would carry this child to full term, and babies arrived early with great regularity.

The only real question in her mind was whether she should ever let Cayetano know. How would he react if he knew what they'd created? Would it enhance the memory of the moments they'd shared, or would it darken that memory forever? Sandra even allowed herself a minute or two to imagine Cayetano coming to Legado to claim the child — and her — as his own. That was folly, of course, something that could never happen, though Sandra was surprised by how much her spirits soared thinking about it.

She'd made up her mind about that as well now. Cayetano would not know about the child that was currently wreaking havoc on her inner workings. Maybe some day, but not at any point when it could complicate things for him. She didn't want that between them.

A knock came on the bathroom door. "Sandra, you're not throwing up again, are you?"

It was her mother. For as long as she could remember, Sandra's mother had always nursed her through illness.

"I'm fine, Mother, thank you."

"Do you want me to get you a cold compress?"

"That won't be necessary. I'll be out in a minute."

"Some tea, then."

"Yes, tea would be lovely."

She heard her mother move away from the door. *You'll make a wonderful grandmother, Madre,* she thought as she washed her face. Then she thought of Sebastian's mother, who would be overjoyed to have a grandchild so soon after the wedding.

Some secrets were best worth keeping.

Chapter 5
Castile, Léon, February

Allie's nose had been pressed up to the car window for so long that Alex wasn't sure she'd be able to dislodge herself. *"Hermoso, muy hermoso,"* she'd said repeatedly, practicing her Spanish, as the car roamed the hills just outside of Castile, Léon's capital city. Alex agreed that the countryside was "beautiful, very beautiful," and he'd always prompted himself to take note of this whenever he got the opportunity, but the effect on Allie was something else entirely. It was as though this land had enchanted her and that she'd willingly gone under its spell.

Some of this, of course, could easily be attributable to Allie's being a city child. Yes, Angélica and he made every effort to get their daughter to the park, they had their beach home in the summer, and at least a third of their vacations involved rigorous outdoor activity. Still, very few of the places they'd visited over the years could match the splendor of Castile's topography, so it wasn't surprising that a kid who spent most of her time weaving through pedestrians on teeming Manhattan streets would find this mesmerizing.

That wasn't all of it, though. As soon as they left the city limits, before Allie's nose had become, perhaps permanently, glued to the window, she'd turned to her parents with a look of such wonderment that Alex was certain that she'd spotted a pegasus or a griffin or one of the other mythological beasts they'd read about over the years. Certainly, it couldn't just be the gazania and poppies that electrified the landscape with their color.

"It's too bad Allie isn't enjoying herself," Angélica said, pushing her shoulder against Alex's.

Alex smiled at his wife. "We really need to teach her to appreciate nature."

Angélica leaned into him, nestling closer, and the two of them watched the landscape pass out the window opposite their daughter. Angélica had required no persuasion to book a flight to Léon for her daughter and herself to join Alex while he worked with the king. When Alex suggested it to her, it almost seemed as though Angélica had been wondering why he hadn't done so sooner. Allie squealed when he told her and mentioned a bit too enthusiastically that she'd be missing tests in both math and language arts. This had actually given Alex pause, but he knew that he couldn't rescind the invitation at that point, and Allie was still at a school age where missing short stretches had few meaningful consequences.

Surprisingly, Alex's mother chose not to join them. Since she was over for dinner several times a week, since she'd always spoken fondly of her visits to Léon, and since she regularly joined them on vacations, it seemed natural that she'd want to come. She'd shut the conversation down instantly, though. Something about not being up for a long flight. There wasn't much logic to this, since she'd recently been back to Legado, but Alex wasn't going to argue. He'd learned a long time ago that pushing his mother to do anything she didn't want to do yielded very little.

Alex had given the tiniest bit of thought against arranging this trip at all, simply because Romeo Ólgar's unpredictability meant that this might not be the best time for his wife and daughter to be in Léon. Alex had been focusing so closely on the prime minister's actions that he'd become somewhat myopic about them. Ultimately, he convinced himself that Ólgar couldn't turn the country upside down instantaneously and, if he did indeed eventually turn the country upside down, this could be the last time for many years that Alex would be able to bring his family for a visit.

And now that they were out in the countryside, away from the crowds and seemingly away from the reach of politics, Alex felt entirely comfortable with his decision. Here it was just good people living quiet lives and, "*Hermoso, muy hermoso.*"

The car pulled onto a manicured lane and, thirty seconds later, into a small gravel parking lot. Allie burst out of the car the moment it stopped, confirming that she could in fact separate herself from the window. She threw her arms open and inhaled deeply. Alex took a little longer to get outside, but when he did he understood instantly why Allie wanted to fill her lungs with the smell of this olive grove. He was tempted to do the same himself. There were few scents as distinctive as olives from Léon. The Italians might believe that they had the best olive oil, and the Spanish might argue the same, but discerning palates knew that the oil from Léon was fruitier and more fragrant than either.

Angélica and Allie would be staying in a guest house on the property tonight. The driver would be taking Alex back for another meeting with the king in a couple of hours. Until then, he would tour the grounds, laugh as Allie cringed at the bitterness of the fruit straight from the tree, join the owner for charcuterie, and revel in his daughter's absolute enjoyment of this place.

Though he hardly needed to be reminded, the vision of this land and Allie's immediate connection to it emphasized that this was a country worth saving. He would do everything he could to help the king accomplish that.

"Dad, why are you standing around?" Allie said, shaking him from his reverie. "We need to go *explore*."

◊ ◊ ◊

New York, 1998

Fernando might have been one of the few people on the planet who calmed down when he was in Manhattan. Alex had been living in New York for seven years now and virtually everyone he knew was amped and feeding off the amphetamine energy that seemed to be pumped into the air here. Not the prince, though. While he was manic and on stage during their European forays, he seemed relaxed and contained when they'd gotten together here. What would he have been like if they'd ever decided to meet in Iowa?

"I like this room," Fernando said as they waited for their appetizers at Lespinasse at the St. Regis Hotel, which was also where Fernando and his entourage was staying. "It feels very European without actually, you know, *being* European."

Alex glanced around at the room's muted tones and soft fabrics. While he was making considerably more money now than he'd ever made before, he still didn't get the opportunity to dine at true four-star places like this terribly often. Of course, he wasn't paying for this meal; Fernando – or more specifically the taxpayers of Léon – was paying.

"I've been here exactly once before after closing a deal. It didn't feel European to me then. It just felt like money. I see what you're saying, though."

Fernando took a long sip of wine and gazed off in the middle distance. Alex guessed that, from Fernando's expression, he wasn't contemplating the gilt overlay in the wainscoting.

"My father is proposing marriage," he said.

"Is that something the people in your country do? It seems a bit unconventional to marry your son, not to mention the fact that he's already married. But at least you don't have to think that he doesn't like you anymore."

Fernando looked at Alex wryly then smiled softly when he saw that Alex too was wearing a wry expression.

"He's proposing *a* marriage. For me. To Katarina Villar."

"Any relation to Hernan Villar?"

"Oldest daughter. The most prized bauble in the billionaire's coffers."

"Well, it sounds better than if your father were trying to marry you off to Villar's second most prized bauble. That would be the holdings in Corfu, no?"

Fernando snorted. "I'd probably be more compatible with the yacht club."

"Are you saying that Ms. Villar lacks personality."

"I'm not, actually. She's extremely smart, she has a deep concern for the welfare of people, particularly children, and she's written at length about the need for us to help the underprivileged all around the world reach their potential."

"She sounds great. Can I marry her?"

"Well, I think you might have hit the nail right on the head there. She *is* great. She's bright and caring and engaged. She's also beautiful, by the way. Did I mention that?"

Alex's brows knitted. "I'm having a difficult time understanding what the problem is here."

"The problem is that none of those adjectives describe me."

"Oh, don't sell yourself short. You're really quite attractive."

Fernando tipped his wine glass in Alex's direction. "If this wine weren't so rare, I'd throw it at you right now."

Alex held up his hands in surrender. "Okay, I get it. Katarina Villar is spectacular, just not your kind of spectacular."

"Now you understand."

Alex wasn't entirely sure that he did. Or rather he wasn't entirely sure that he understood what Fernando's "kind of spectacular" might be. In the time that they'd been friends, Alex had never known Fernando to have more than a couple of dates with any one woman and, while the tabloids regularly linked him with actresses, supermodels, and socialites, Fernando didn't seem interested in pursuing any of these relationships. Now that he thought about it, Alex couldn't recall a single conversation they'd had about women that involved Fernando expressing any preference at all.

"So, what are you going to do about it?"

"I'm contemplating my options as we speak."

"Might one of those options be actually marrying Katarina Villar?"

"That's the strongest option, I'm afraid. Hence all the contemplation."

Fernando finished his glass and poured himself another. The wine was getting rarer by the second.

Fernando brightened. "Did I mention that I got to accompany the education secretary to this year's European Schools Council conference in Paris?"

Alex inched forward in his chair. "You did not. What was it like?"

"Alternately energizing and enervating. There are some interesting programs being tested, especially in Finland, which is a bit of a surprise because their education system has always been so uninspiring. Some of these programs are worth monitoring. At the same time, I must have listened to four presentations about the need to collect more data. There's lots of talk about a worldwide standardized test coming in a few years. Sounds dreadful. What could possibly go wrong?"

"Not a fan of data?"

"Not in this field. Maybe in yours, but not in mine."

Alex knew that data only provided so much insight, even in his field. That was why it was so critical that he be able to read the principals in any deal at a much deeper level. Alex supposed that was even truer in education, but what he found most fascinating about Fernando's comment was Fernando's referring to that particular field as his.

"Explain this to me. I'm not sure I'm following you."

Fernando leaned toward him, shifting his entire body forward, and spent from that moment until their entrees were cleared presenting his perspective on the role of schools, a vision that involved understanding each child's needs at a granular level while employing a vast array of educational applications to simultaneously address that child's strengths and weaknesses. It all sounded unrealistically ambitious to Alex, but it was exciting to see Fernando so animated. Earlier, Fernando had described Katarina Villar as a woman full of passion and commitment, and he'd said that the same words did not apply to him. Here, though, he was contradicting that notion.

And then the wait staff took away their plates, and it was as though they'd accidentally carted off Fernando's enthusiasm with the dirty dishes.

"When the conference was over, the education secretary thanked me for tagging along. He said it was great to have a 'rock star' with the Léon delegation. In other words, he reminded me that my only function in life is a ceremonial one."

The pivot from engagement to resignation was so swift that it might have taken Alex's breath away if he hadn't seen this sort of thing from Fernando before. In the past, he might have tried to convince Fernando to look at the situation from a different perspective, maybe even suggesting that the prince make a formal presentation of his observations to the education secretary. That approach had never succeeded for Alex in the past, and Fernando's body language suggested that he'd be even less receptive to it tonight.

"It's time for more drinking at a different venue," Fernando said. "I assume you've discovered some excruciatingly trendy spots for us to while away the evening."

Alex had of course done his research. At this point, he had a section in his diary specifically dedicated to the hottest bars and clubs in any city where he might find himself with Fernando.

"I have a few suggestions. However, I'm not sure how much of the evening I'm going to be able to while away. I have a hugely important meeting in the morning."

Fernando adjusted himself in his chair. It was though he literally expanded in preparation for a night of oblivion. "Foolish talk, Alejandro Soberano. No meeting is more important than this – and every meeting is better attended hung over."

They left and headed to the East Village where Alex had heard about a club that offered the combination of grittiness and exclusivity that seemed to entertain Fernando the most. Four hours, two bottles of Cristal, and a half-dozen celebrity sightings (not to mention the countless times Fernando was recognized) later, Alex ushered Fernando into his car before hailing a taxi for himself. Before they parted, they made plans to meet for dinner again that night.

Alex managed to have a productive day and even conceded that Fernando might have a point about hangovers and meetings since things had gone extremely well. That night, he showed up at the St. Regis at 7:30 and took the elevator up to Fernando's suite. As usual, Esteban, a member of the prince's detail, was at the door.

"He's not in there," Esteban said when Alex greeted him.

"We're supposed to go out to dinner. Do you know when he'll be back?"

"I'm not at liberty to say."

That was the most officious thing Alex had ever heard come from Esteban's mouth. "Esteban, it's me. Has there been a change in plans?"

For another moment, the guard stared ahead stiffly. Then his shoulders slumped. "I'm not at liberty to say, because I don't know where he is. He was asleep until noon and then asked for one of our team to go out to get him a cranberry muffin from a bakery in SoHo. Somewhere between then and when Carlos came back with the muffin the prince disappeared."

"Fernando slipped past your entire detail?"

"As you can imagine, this is worrying on a number of levels."

Alex thought back to their first conversation at dinner last night. Could one of the "options" Fernando had been contemplating been vanishing? Would he even know how to vanish?

"Who's looking for him?"

"Everyone but me. I got stuck with door duty."

Getting away from his entire detail would have taken an extreme level of ingenuity. If Fernando were this committed to doing something, Alex was concerned about how far he'd be willing to carry it.

"What can I do to help?" he said.

Esteban shook his head slowly. "We actually have a plan in place for something like this. The king insisted. We're implementing that plan now."

"Well, if I can be of any assistance, let me know."

Esteban simply nodded. When it was clear that the conversation was over, Alex turned back toward the elevator. He wondered where his friend was right now. And how long it would be before he saw him again.

◊ ◊ ◊

Iguaçu Falls, Brazil, 1971

This was the first time Sandra had been on South American soil with Cayetano. Getting away at all without Sebastian and the children was difficult, and it had become prohibitively so to travel to another part of the world entirely. Sandra had to face the possibility that this would mean the end to her rare, cherished moments with the man she loved, but he surprised her by suggesting this remarkable spot in Brazil. After reuniting last night and spending the entirety of the morning in bed, they'd ventured out to the waterfall this afternoon, standing in awe of its scale and indignation. These falls would not bow to anything man or nature could provide.

"Does this make you feel small, my love," Cayetano said as they watched.

"Not at all. It makes me feel mighty to be part of a world where this exists."

He'd wrapped an arm around her at that point and they shared a long, silent moment, Sandra allowing the power of being in this place with this man to surge through her. She'd made every effort to resolve that they could never be more than what they were right here, but it was at times like these that she couldn't help but imagine a world in which being with Cayetano was an everyday experience.

They left the falls about fifteen minutes later, holding hands as they took the car back to their hotel. Sandra could only guess at what Cayetano was thinking during this drive, but she sensed that, like her, he was considering the scale of what they'd just experienced – and maybe even considering the scale of what they were going through together.

They hadn't taken much time for conversation in the twenty hours or so they'd been together so far. When they got back now, though she would have gladly opted for his arms, they decided to spend some time poolside.

"Is he treating you well?" Cayetano said as a waiter brought them drinks.

"Sebastian is a very kind man. He's good with the children, especially our daughter, and he's taken to spending most of his evenings at home."

"Does he love you?"

"I think he might, at least by his own definition. I think he has an inclination that there are places in my heart that he'll never reach, and I think he does his best to care for me in ways that he can. In exchange, I show appreciation when he takes me dancing or to the opera or stands by my side at the endless number of parties to which we're invited. He knows I'd rather be anywhere else than those."

"And he has no concerns about you pursuing your career?"

Sandra laughed. "Why on earth would he? My professional success allows him to do the thing he most wants in the world — to not work. Did I mention that he's taken up painting? Acrylics. He fashions himself a modern-day Mondrian, who himself seems to be having something of a renaissance these days. At least that's what Sebastian says."

"So, he doesn't feel threatened at all having a commodities dealer for a wife."

Sandra tilted her head toward Cayetano. "Sometimes when you ask about my career I get the impression that *you* would feel threatened having a commodities dealer for a wife."

Cayetano's eyes flashed with surprise. "Me? Why would that ever be so?" He reached out for her hand. "No, my love, I am not saying that at all. It's just an awfully evolved stance for someone like your husband."

Sandra shrugged. "It is convenient for him to be evolved. And now that he's an artist, it even fits with his persona. Artists are supposed to be on the forefront of social trends, no?"

"I suppose so."

Sandra admitted that her career was convenient for both Sebastian and herself. Not only did it provide their household with a comfortable income — something his prestigious family could not do — but it gave her an alibi for these rare getaways. Right now, she was supposed to be at a commodities conference in Venezuela.

"Does your wife ever wish she could be something like a commodities dealer?" she said.

"I can honestly say I would be stunned if she'd ever given a moment's thought to commodities. Unless, of course, one considers such commodities as potty seats and children's overalls."

Sandra smiled at this. She was glad that the days of potty seats were now in her recent past. Cayetano had married the year after she'd married Sebastian, and his boy and girl were younger. "She wants to be a good mother."

Cayetano nodded. "I think she's taken to motherhood. Brilliantly, actually." He furrowed his brows. "That's allowed, isn't it?"

"Of course it's allowed. As long as it's from desire and not constraint."

"I'm glad you feel that way. I didn't want you to think less of me because I wasn't married to a modern woman."

"There's a certain amount of irony in you and me having this conversation, isn't there?"

Cayetano tilted his head back and let the sun wash his face for a moment. "Yes, there is." He leaned toward her and took both of her hands. "You know that what we're doing isn't an affair, don't you?"

Sandra squeezed his hands tightly. "I do know that."

"It's . . . indefinable."

"We don't need to define it. We just need to capture it."

He moved closer and kissed her deeply. Sandra had felt several kisses like this one since last night, but each conveyed so much that it never failed to surprise her.

"I think I'd like to capture it in a more private venue," he said.

"I think I would like that as well."

They rose together and walked slowly, dreamily toward the hotel's elevators. *We just need to capture it.* Sandra had been trying to do so, and she would keep continuing to try until they parted the morning after next, never knowing which of these stolen days would be their last.

Chapter 6
Castile, February

Alex didn't need to ask if Angélica and Allie had enjoyed themselves on this trip to Léon. His wife's expression and his daughter's animated recitations of the day's events made it apparent that they had. Though Alex had spent much of their time in the country working with the king, not to mention staying connected to the home office and to various interests around the globe, he'd managed to share a number of meals and excursions with his family. He'd noticed immediately that there was something unrushed about these experiences, a sense of flow that he'd rarely felt on other vacations. Maybe it was simply because this was a bonus vacation; there was none of the pressure on this trip that often accompanied those that took months of planning. Or maybe it was something that had more to do with where they were and what they were doing.

They'd be heading back to New York this afternoon. Allie had been lobbying for one more trip into the countryside, but that wasn't likely to happen. Maybe they could take a circuitous route to the airport that would allow her to see the rolling hills outside of Castile a final time before their departure, but that was likely to be the best that Alex could offer. It tickled him that his daughter had so completely fallen in love with this place. Léon was home to some excellent universities. Maybe college or postgrad here was a possibility for her.

After all, he'd spent his college years as a foreign student, and things had worked out pretty well for him.

Alex had awoken early, planning as always to respond to email from his office sent after he'd gone to bed and to reach out to a few people in Asia. When he got to the common room in their suite where he'd kept his laptop, though, he found Allie propped up on the couch looking at her own laptop.

"Morning, Dad," she said.

He walked over and kissed her on the top of her head. "Morning, Babe. Why are you up so early?"

"I couldn't sleep. I *really* don't want to leave – and, yes, I know we have to. I've been watching stuff on YouTube. Have you heard of this guy Romeo Ólgar?"

Alex chuckled. He'd told Allie that he was working with the king on a very important project, but he hadn't given her many specifics, not wanting anything to color her experience of Léon and knowing that any conversation that involved Ólgar was going to require showing Allie the nation's more complicated side.

"Well, yes. He's the main reason we're here, actually."

"He has a very weird aura."

Alex's eyes widened at this pronouncement. Alex had taught Allie how to read auras by the time she was three, so this part of what she'd said wasn't surprising at all. What was surprising was that she'd been able to read Ólgar's aura when Alex himself had not. And then there was the matter of her doing this through a video. Alex had never known anyone who could read auras in any way other than being in the presence of the person he was reading. He looked at the screen now and saw no indication of an electromagnetic field around any of the people in the image, even as he adjusted his eyes the way he had during his meeting with the prime minister.

"You can see Ólgar's aura?"

"Yep. And like I said it's very weird. It's like it's every color at once and then it's like no color at all. You don't see this kind of thing too much."

"Does that mean you've seen something like this before?"

"You see all kinds of things on the internet, Dad."

"Something tells me I don't actually want to know the answer to this question, but what kinds of things are you talking about in this case?"

She smirked at him. She'd been smirking at him more often lately, and Alex didn't want to get used to this becoming a normal thing.

"Don't freak out," she said. "I've been trying to remember where else I saw something like this. I've only been reading online auras for a few months, so it couldn't have been that long ago. I'm pretty sure I saw it on this guy who pranked people into hurting themselves. Caryn showed his videos to me at school once. I thought they were pretty mean, but lots of other people thought they were hilarious. I tried to find them today, and it looks like they were taken down."

"I've been working with the king to do something similar with Ólgar. Maybe I should contact YouTube. What's your reading on the aura?"

"Not totally sure. You know when I said that his aura seemed to have every color in it? They're all there, piled one on top of the other, but they're all really muddy. Like the grungiest version of all of these colors."

"Romeo Ólgar is not a very nice guy, Babe."

"Yeah, I kinda figured that."

"The question is *how* not nice he is."

Rather than responding, Allie stared deeper into the screen.

"Tell me about this video aura reading thing," Alex said.

Allie looked away from the image and toward her father. "It isn't just videos. I can do it with any picture online. Here, see this one?"

Allie opened a tab that showed the Twitter feed of the star of one of her favorite teen television shows. Then she clicked on a tweet to enlarge the photograph of the same star on a red carpet.

"Lots of green in there. She's definitely doing better. There was so much gray in her aura a few weeks ago after she broke up with Clint Blake."

"You're blowing my mind a little bit here, Allie."

She smiled up at him. "That's my job, Dad."

"And you do it brilliantly. Hey, if we leave for the airport a little early, we'll be able to take the long way around so you can take some more pictures of the flowers. Sound good?"

"Sounds *great*. Thanks for bringing me here, Dad. I really like Léon. I'll finish packing my stuff."

◊ ◊ ◊

Alex was still processing his early-morning conversation with Allie and all that it implied when he went to say goodbye to the king. As soon as he entered the room, IV rose to embrace him.

"We're doing important work here, Alex. I can't begin to tell you how much I appreciate your contribution to it."

Alex wasn't entirely sure what his contribution had actually been. They'd worked with a team to study the prime minister's public actions and policy statements, debriefed dozens of friendly staff members within the Ólgar administration, and game-planned a number of scenarios regarding Ólgar's possible next moves. Alex had never felt as though he had the skillset to be a politician, but he knew he had real value as a strategist, so he'd spent most of these sessions focusing on plans that were within the king's direct authority that could help blunt the prime minister's effect on the nation and their closest allies.

"I wish I could have contributed more, sir."

"I trust that you will as we continue to work our way through this."

"You have my private line. I'm going to be underwater with corporate initiatives over the next month or so, and I'll be playing catch-up with my staff, but if I can't get back to you right away, I'll do so as soon as I possibly can."

The king clapped him on the shoulder, his large hand pressing its weight. "Léon needs you, Alex."

Of course, Alex wanted to help — because he cared about the king and his son, because the people of Léon mattered to him, and because he had very real concerns about what Ólgar could do both in and out of the country. At the same time, he knew that this could easily become an obsession or an all-consuming campaign. And while he'd finally gotten the upper management of his company to the point where he felt the corporation could run comfortably without him for a stretch of time, he was not convinced that the same would be true if that stretch ran more than a couple of weeks.

"You can count on me to do everything I have the capacity of doing."

The king hugged him again at that point, almost certainly not hearing what Alex was trying to say.

◊ ◊ ◊

Later, on the plane, while Angélica and Allie dozed, Alex took himself into the deep meditative state that allowed him to reach out to Vidente.

"Our little girl is a prodigy," he said. "She's getting readings I didn't even think were possible."

"You're a good teacher."

"I'd love to take credit for this, but I think this is all her. It's as though she's working with a next-generation operating system."

"You know how I abhor high-tech jargon, *bisnieto*."

"Yes, sorry."

"I understand your point, though. Allie is taking things further. This is cause for celebration."

"I suppose it is. But there's more. She was able to see colors in Romeo Ólgar's aura."

"She was? But not even I could see them."

Alex found that amusing, a reminder that even in the afterlife his great-grandmother's pride remained vital.

"She wasn't sure how to interpret what she was seeing. She said it was like all colors and no color at once and that all of the colors were 'muddy.'"

Vidente didn't respond for several seconds. "If that's true, she might have discovered something about this man that should concern you deeply."

"*Everything* about this man concerns me deeply."

"This should concern you the most. I should talk to Allie about this directly, but if she's seeing what I think she might be seeing, Ólgar has a very rare level of control over himself and his environment. The consequences could be dire."

"You sound like the king. I think he'd prefer it if I took a sabbatical to work exclusively on countermeasures."

Vidente paused again. "Is that an option?"

"No, it is not an option."

"You might want to make it one."

This was not at all the way Alex thought this conversation was going to go.

"Vidente, I have promised to help Léon to the fullest extent I can. But I can only take so much time away from the company. I have many responsibilities, and Léon is not chief among them, no matter how much I care."

"I understand, *bisnieto*. Your responsibilities are vast. Understand this, though: you've been given this particular responsibility as well, and it might indeed be your greatest."

Alex's great-grandmother had never spoken to him with such portent in her voice before. Even in this state suspended between levels of consciousness, it gave him chills.

◊ ◊ ◊

New York, 1998

"Please hold for King Alfonso."

Since he'd never gotten a call from the king before, Alex probably should have been surprised to hear those words on his phone line. However, he had no doubts over why the man was calling. Fernando had disappeared and the plan his security team had in place wasn't working.

Alex had checked in with Fernando's detail several times last night and he stopped by the St. Regis again this morning before going to his office. Esteban, with whom he'd developed something of a relationship since Fernando and he had started sojourning together, let him know that their search had turned up nothing and that there was no suggestion that Fernando had come to any harm. Other Léon agents were now searching for Fernando outside of the city and even outside of the country.

"Thank you for taking my call, Alex," the king said when he got on the line.

"Of course, Your Majesty."

"I assume you know why I'm calling."

"I'm afraid I do. No news?"

"None at all. My son has sometimes been difficult to track down in the past, but there's never been anything like this. You were with him the night before last, weren't you?"

"I was. Quite far into the night, actually."

The king let out a sigh. "Yes, I'm not surprised. What was he like?"

"It was like we had two entirely different evenings. At dinner, he was contemplative. More than I've ever seen him before. Almost wistful, which is an emotion I never would have attached to Fernando. Then we left the restaurant and went to a club and he was the Prince Fernando we've all seen in public."

"The Tabloid Prince."

Alex had heard the nickname before, mostly on their European jaunts. Such a label would have horrified Alex if it had been connected to himself, but Fernando seemed to cultivate it and revel in it.

"Yes, Your Majesty. As thoughtful and reflective as he'd been while we were having dinner, he was boisterous and larger than life once we got to the club."

The image of Fernando grinding with three mini-skirted women came to mind. Did the prince seem just a little more immersed in his public persona that night, or had the events that followed revised Alex's memory?

"Tell me more about your conversation over dinner."

"A lot of it revolved around Katarina Villar."

Another sigh. "I'm guessing he wasn't gushing with excitement over the prospective match."

"I wouldn't use that term, Your Majesty, no."

"Do you know anything about Katarina Villar?"

"A little bit more since the other night."

"Do you see anything wrong with what I'm proposing?"

"It's really not my place to say. However, I will say that Fernando's reticence is more about the circumstances than about the woman."

"You mean he doesn't want his father making these decisions for him."

"He didn't specifically say that, but I would guess that's part of it. I do think it's possible that the whole idea of marrying and giving up his lifestyle might have caused him to bolt. Not that he gave any indication of this. What he did came as a complete surprise to me."

The line was quiet for several seconds.

"Alex, I'm worried about him. Do you have any idea where he might have gone?"

"I assume you have people searching his favorite spots."

"At least those of which I know. Your insight on this would be welcome. I could really use your help here, Alex. Your friend needs you."

Alex wasn't entirely sure that was true. Maybe what Fernando needed more than anything else was to step away for a short while. By necessity, he'd have to change his lifestyle dramatically to stay under the radar. Perhaps that in itself would prove beneficial. However, Alex knew he couldn't say that to Fernando's worried father.

"I'll help in any way I can, Your Majesty."

"Thank you, Alex. It's easy to understand why my son cares about you so much. We're gathering as much intelligence as we can. May I get back to you in a day or so?"

"Yes, of course."

"Thank you. Alex, my son and I don't always agree on things, but I'd like to think he knows that I want the best for him. Running away from his life is not the best for him. We'll speak again soon."

Alex hung up the phone and took a deep breath. Fernando's eluding his security detail and disappearing somewhere in the world — whether it was a mile or five thousand miles from here — had required planning. If he'd gone through that much effort, he would have put an equal amount of planning into making sure he could stay away as long as he chose.

Finding Fernando was not going to be easy.

◊ ◊ ◊

Iguaçu Falls, Brazil, 1971

Sandra awoke to find Cayetano staring at the ceiling. She kissed his shoulder and he smiled over at her.

"Have you been up long?" she said.

"Did you know that in the middle of the night you can hear the sound of the falls all the way from here?"

"I assume that means you were awake in the middle of the night. Is everything okay?"

Cayetano didn't respond immediately. Instead, he looked up at the ceiling again so intently that Sandra found herself looking up there as well. At last, he flipped onto his side to face her. When he did, she saw the kind of devotion in his eyes that she'd only seen when they were making love.

"I've been thinking a great deal about my marriage, Sandra."

Sandra recoiled a bit emotionally. It wasn't as though she ever forgot that both of them were married to other people, but she'd managed to keep the presence of those marriages at a distance for most of their time in Brazil.

"Not the words one wants to hear when in bed with her lover."

He smiled again, this time sadder. "I can't keep doing it, Sandra."

She closed her eyes. She assumed that they would have this conversation at some point but had been hoping it wouldn't be during this trip. She'd collected such fulfilling memories the past few days.

Cayetano propped himself up on one arm. "I don't want to keep living with a part-time version of you and me."

The declaration caught her off guard since she had already begun to prepare herself for a very different talk. "What are you saying?"

"I'm saying what I'd already admitted to myself and what has only become clearer to me while we've been here: what you and I share is too precious to be an occasional thing. How many people truly get what we have? When deep love is gifted to you, you can't refuse the gift."

Sandra could feel her heart beating in her chest. "I'm so unsure what to say."

"I understand, my love. I think I know what you're thinking. You're thinking that my leaving my wife will have terrible consequences. That I will be doing damage that I can't undo. That I will be hurting people who don't deserve to be hurt. It's so like you to be concerned about these things. I'm concerned about them as well, of course. How could I not be? They have kept me up most of the night. Most of the night before last as well, to be truthful.

"But I am ready, Sandra. I've come to understand that the pain of not having you is far greater than all of the pain to be caused by doing the things I need to do to be with you."

Sandra found that she was utterly unprepared for this conversation. She'd so completely convinced herself that circumstances would never allow Cayetano and she to be together that she'd always considered any notion of a more permanent relationship to be fanciful. When, minutes earlier, she was bracing for him to tell her that they could no longer be lovers, she found herself calm if a bit mournful; they'd come to the inevitable and she would cherish what they'd been able to share forever. This, though, left her feeling as though a surprise visitor had just burst through the door.

"How could we ever consider this?" she said.

"In my heart, the question is no longer considering it — it is acting upon it. I've been thinking about this endlessly for hours. In my head, I've had the conversation with my wife, my children . . . my father. These have not been easy conversations in my mind, and I'm sure they will be exponentially more difficult conversations in reality. But at the end of it all, there is us."

"I think you might be underestimating the complications and the consequences. For both of us."

Cayetano touched her face tenderly. "Of course, there would be consequences for you. I know you feel affection, if not love, for your husband, and that you appreciate the relationship he has with your children. There would be much to work out for both of us. But you want this, don't you, Sandra? It's impossible for me to believe that you don't when I think about how we've spoken, how we've held each other, how we've loved these past few days."

Asking Sandra if she wanted this was akin to asking her if she wanted to be taller or French. She'd always considered it such an impossibility that she never really considered it at all, at least not seriously.

And what did she think now that Cayetano was suggesting that it could be a possibility? There was little question that he was the great love in her life. She'd long acknowledged that he was likely to be the only true experience of romantic love she would ever have, and she was thankful that it had been such an overwhelming experience. But lives were about so much more than love, weren't they? They were about children having access to their fathers. They were about walking through a community without whispers. They were about hard-won careers that might not be winnable twice. Sandra had accomplished more with her business than anyone ever believed she could, and she knew that this was much more than a substitute for a great marriage. She was at least as defined by her entrepreneurial success as she could ever imagine being by love.

"There isn't a doubt in my mind that I will always love you, Cayetano. And I want what we've had this weekend – what we've always had when we're together – more, I think, than breath. But I think what we have right now might be everything we are meant to have. It isn't just about how difficult it would be for us to extricate ourselves from our marriages. It's about all of the damage we would do, maybe permanent damage, to people who matter to us. We don't have the right to inflict this damage."

"We don't have the right to love?"

Sandra moved into his arms, glad that he still welcomed her there. "Yes, we absolutely have the right to love. But not at all costs. I would like nothing more than to be able to wake up beside you every single day, but maybe neither of us would feel that way if we had to endure enormous tribulation to have that opportunity."

Cayetano locked eyes with her. "I can't give you up, my love."

She kissed his forehead. "Nor can I give you up. Let's take a secret vow right now, one that carries with it even greater commitment than our wedding vows. Let us vow that we will find a time every year to be what we are in this room. One weekend a year when nothing matters but us. I think I might be able to live with that if I always knew I had another weekend to look forward to."

He squeezed her tighter. "Can that possibly be enough?"

"We will make it enough. Forever."

Chapter 7
Castile, March

Alex was back in Léon three weeks after he'd come home with his wife and daughter. His chief operating officer and chief revenue officer were up in arms about this − there were deals on the table − but Alex had taken the king's entreaty and Vidente's somewhat cryptic exhortation to heart. His adopted home needed him, and Alex simply couldn't ignore that, even with so much pending business at hand. And maybe it wasn't the worst thing for the company to be challenged in this way. Alex was many, many years from retirement, but effective succession plans took an extremely long time to orchestrate properly. Perhaps this situation when more of his executive staff was forced to step up would be instructive, giving Alex a better sense of who might someday be able to steer the direction of the company full-time before Allie was of age to take over.

While contemplating the value of his top management was a useful exercise, at this very moment, the bigger question was whether he himself could actually have any value in Léon. As much of a public figure as Ólgar had become, it was surprisingly difficult to get much background information on him beyond what little was made available to the press. If this was even true given the king's resources, finding the "poison pill" in Ólgar's history might prove entirely elusive. Ólgar had been relatively anonymous until about ten years ago, staying out of government and holding down a number of mid-level management positions at a number of companies, always leaving in less than two years. After that, he seemed to come out of nowhere, winning a council seat in the Hermenegildo region, which was the birthplace of El General, leading Alex to wonder if there was something in the Hermenegildo water that caused people to have outsized thoughts about the extent of their rule. Four years later, he was named Minister of the Interior, which surprised many given his limited political experience at that point. He used that platform to project himself as a man of the people, fighting to improve living conditions in many of Léon's poorest communities and rallying the downtrodden at every turn. When he chose to run for prime minister, the belief was that he was doing this at least a dozen years too soon for such a position and that the voters would reject him because of this. However, the base he'd built and the public's worry about an unsteady economy had swept him into office. When Ólgar instantly began to turn his back on the voters who'd elevated him, buyer's remorse ran rampant. At that point, though, it was too late. Which was how Alex found himself in Léon trying to be somewhat useful.

Just before lunch on his third day there, Alex called home. If he'd planned things properly, he'd get a few precious minutes on the phone with Allie before she had to leave for school.

"Hey, Babe. I hope I'm not messing up the time you need to get ready for the day," he said when Angélica handed their daughter the phone.

"No, I'm all set. Mom doesn't feel the need to have 'quality time' with me first thing in the morning the way you do, so I'm already dressed and finished with breakfast. I've just been looking at stuff on my computer."

Alex chuckled at the way Allie had phrased their morning ritual. Angélica had built her writing schedule around being finished for the day by the time Allie returned from school.

They had the opportunity to do over the course of hours what he only had that little window in the morning to do, so of course Angélica would focus on efficiency over connection at the start of the day.

"Well, we don't have to have our 'quality time' in the morning if you feel that it would get you off to a better start."

"No, that's okay. Are you still trying to figure out that muddy guy?"

Alex again smiled at his daughter's phrasing. "Yeah, the muddy guy. He's a puzzle."

"I totally get it. A few minutes ago, I was watching him speaking to reporters. It was really interesting: the all-color aura was only there when he started. As soon as he began to answer questions, it was the no-color thing all the time."

Alex's senses tingled. "That is interesting. If I had someone from the king's staff send you some more press conference videos, do you think you could see if he always does that?"

"Yeah, of course."

"That would be really helpful. Maybe you should be here, and I should be taking your test on fractions tomorrow."

"You got a deal. I'll have Mom book my flight."

Alex laughed. "I really wish we could do that. I think we're going to have to stick with the original plan, though. I'll make sure the videos are waiting for you when you get home today. Meanwhile, you remember the division trick with fractions, right?"

"Got it covered, Dad."

"I knew you would. Love you."

"Love you, too."

Alex still had a few minutes before he needed to go down for lunch, and he took that time to incorporate what Allie had just told him into his work on Ólgar. If the prime minister was indeed able to manipulate his aura, what was this doing to the way the people in the room perceived him? Was his blanking his aura making him impenetrable or simply neutral? Was that why there was often so little consensus about his messages? This was going to require much further exploration, assuming that Allie found the same thing in the other press conference videos.

For the first time in years, Alex remembered a trip he'd taken to China back in his MIT days in the eighties. He'd been flown to Beijing to serve as the assistant to six MIT economists during a secret mission being held in preparation for the Hong Kong hand-over from the UK to China in 1997. Those sessions were all about adapting long-embedded negotiation techniques to a much more modern culture. Hong Kong and China could not have been further apart ideologically at that point, and the Chinese officials knew that their usual approaches to gaining cooperation weren't going to work. The tools developed during those sessions took time to refine, and they certainly weren't without glitches, but it was the first instance that Alex had seen of one culture achieving such great influence over a profoundly different one without the use of force. Alex hadn't had much reason to access these tools over the years, but might there be something applicable here? Was it possible to *nudge* Ólgar closer to the center?

That night, Alex had dinner with Fernando and his wife. Alex would have been perfectly happy eating whatever the palace's inspired culinary staff came up with, but Fernando insisted on closing a local restaurant for his private dining instead.

"What do they do well here?" Alex said after they'd been handed their menus.

Fernando leaned toward him. "What they do best is keep the doors closed to outsiders."

Alex chuckled. "I'm a little curious about the closed-restaurant thing. I thought you liked to do all of your consumption in public."

Fernando offered a half-smile. "Luciana prefers privacy when we dine together."

Alex glanced over at the princess, who offered him the same half-smile. Alex remembered Luciana's smile on the day she married Fernando ten years earlier. Very definitely a full smile that day, one that radiated throughout the church and, within minutes, throughout Léon and beyond. She was the luminescent social reformer who had managed to perform an unimaginable feat of social reformation – getting the Tabloid Prince to settle down. The media lauded her even as they continued to portray Fernando as cartoonish, and even the Internet had been generous about her accomplishments. Still, she saved nearly all of her public appearances for her causes; the cameras stayed off during most of the time she spent with the children and her husband.

"The best dishes come from the plancha here," she said plainly.

Alex nodded toward that section of the menu. "Thank you for that advice."

"So how are things going with my dad?" Fernando said.

"Slowly. Ólgar is a tough man to read."

"Maybe we shouldn't worry about him as much as we are."

Alex put down his menu, surprised by the comment. "If anything, I think we might not be worrying about him enough. People outside of the country are very concerned, and that's not good for Léon. They're beginning to wonder about the wisdom of doing business here. That's going to begin to have an effect on the nation's economy – which could open a door for Ólgar making further inroads with his political agenda."

Fernando scoffed. "Sometimes I wonder if Ólgar's agenda is really all that much different from the status quo."

Luciana put a hand on her husband's arm. "You don't really mean that, Fernando."

He looked downward toward the table, then sideways toward Alex, and finally toward his wife. "No, I suppose I don't. I've just begun to wonder if the world doesn't move in its own direction, regardless of where its leaders try to steer it."

"I don't think you want to use Ólgar as a test subject for that theory," Alex said. "He's already done things that are shifting the conversation about Léon. Given this country's not-so-distant history, you don't want the conversation to shift in this way."

Fernando grunted and reached for his wine glass. "I'm just finding all of this . . . distasteful."

"Ólgar, or our attempts to neutralize him?"

"Both?"

Luciana again put a hand on Fernando's arm, a gesture he barely seemed to notice.

"I think it might be good for everyone to step away from the state of Léon for a few hours," she said. "Why don't we order some prawns and some olives while we decide what we want to eat?"

Fernando brought the menu closer to him. "Luciana's right. Talk of state matters darkens me, and none of us needs me any darker."

"Not to mention that you've chosen an excellent wine and darkness will diminish it."

A visage of The Tabloid Prince flickered across Fernando's face for an instant then quickly receded. "Yes, I brought three bottles from my own cellar. I'm glad you're enjoying it. We can tap into the restaurant's considerable wine list later, though I can tell you for a fact that you won't find anything this good there."

Alex noticed another half-smile on Luciana's face.

◊ ◊ ◊

New York, 1998

"Thank you, Terrence. If you hear anything, please give me a call."

Alex had said something similar in the last twenty-four hours to nearly a dozen acquaintances he had in common with Fernando. He'd cast that net as far as it would go. Terrence, for example, had rented the two of them a yacht for a discreet party about a year earlier, and Alex had had no communication with the man either before or after. If he kept going along these lines, he'd soon be calling the valet that parked Fernando's car on their last trip to Monaco.

Alex had to give it to Fernando. The prince had orchestrated his disappearance masterfully. It wasn't easy in this age for someone – let alone a celebrity – to drop completely out of sight. Given how little effort Fernando seemed to put into everything else in his life, it was surprising that he could commit to the work necessary to pull this off. Doing this obviously mattered to him. Perhaps that boded well for the point when Fernando discovered a more productive pursuit.

For now, though, it complicated matters for Alex considerably. While Alex believed that Fernando's taking a moderately lengthy break from being Prince Fernando might very well be a good thing, Alex had committed to King Alfonso that he would make every effort to find the king's son. One might argue that making a dozen futile phone calls constituted "every effort," but Alex was certain that the king wouldn't feel that way and, realistically, neither did Alex. The question, however, was what the next move might be, assuming the parking valet option was probably not a viable one.

Meanwhile, the media was beginning to get the sense that something was amiss in the royal palace. The one loose end Fernando had forgotten to tie up before he disappeared was an interview he'd had scheduled with a British teen magazine for two days after he'd taken off. When Fernando wasn't available for the interview, someone in his press office flubbed and said the prince was "inaccessible." This led the magazine to start poking around, and now more substantial publications were asking questions. Some were suggesting that the prince was in the midst of a "lost weekend," the kind of lengthy drunken bender that had been ascribed to pop stars for decades. That sort of thing was unlikely to put a dent in Fernando's reputation, since he was already known as a world-class partier. However, that narrative wasn't going to hold if Fernando remained unavailable to the media for much longer.

Once again, Alex wondered what Fernando was hoping to accomplish with this disappearance. Was he sending a message to his father? In all likelihood, if that were the case, he'd return on his own soon, probably in the next week. Fernando had to know that, even without the teen magazine error, the media would start to question his unavailability rather quickly — he was in the news all the time, after all — and start to develop their own theories. On the other hand, if Fernando's plan was to abdicate his responsibilities to the throne, he might not care what anyone else had to say or be concerned about having access to his riches — or even his identity — in the future. That would make him exponentially harder to find.

Alex looked at the pink phone message slips his assistant had dropped on his desk fifteen minutes earlier. There were eight, including at least two from the same client. Alex wasn't going to be able to prioritize his search for Fernando over his job for much longer today. One of the things that had contributed to his quick ascendancy at the company had been his utter dedication to his work, the kind of dedication that manifested in giving all of his clients his highest level of attention. He couldn't say he'd been providing that kind of attention the past couple of days, and if this went on much longer, it was likely to start to show. That would have an unwelcome effect on Alex's near-term plans and do perhaps lasting damage to his long-term ones.

He would make one more call. Brittany Howell was an English academic that Fernando had lunched with during a trip he took with Alex to London. Fernando had made it very clear that Alex wasn't invited to the lunch and, when Alex joked afterward about the prince's "afternoon delight," Fernando made it stridently obvious that Howell was not a romantic partner. A bit more playful probing identified why this was the case: Fernando had a huge level of respect for

Brittany Howell, which by extension disqualified her from a place in his bed. Alex hadn't thought much about Howell since then, but it dawned on him now that Fernando might have let the professor in on his plans. It was worth a try. Especially since all other leads had proven fruitless and Alex hated having nothing to show for so much work.

◊ ◊ ◊

Cap D'Antibes, 1981

Cayetano wasn't in bed when Sandra awoke, and she could hear his voice on the phone in the other room. She didn't need to eavesdrop to know what was going on: he was taking care of business. Just as he had on numerous occasions yesterday. During their time together, he was as attentive and passionate as always on their annual escapes, but for the first time Cayetano had booked interruptions to their stolen days. Forty-five minutes yesterday morning and another hour-and-a-half just before dinner. She could only imagine what time he got up this morning so he could be on the phone while she slept.

There was a certain amount of irony associated with Cayetano's being pulled in multiple directions on this trip. This year, they'd decided to return to the place of their first meeting. It was a complicated enterprise logistically, but Sandra embraced the idea because she was feeling somewhat nostalgic for the unbridled romance of those first days in France. The children didn't need her as much anymore, and she and her husband had only ever sparked on the dance floor, a place they had begun to visit less and less frequently. Her one weekend a year with Cayetano offered her essential sustenance, but she sensed that a return to Cap D'Antibes would help her to feel things that she might have been beginning to forget. Maybe a visit to the bar where they first met would refresh her with the wonder of their initial conversation and this would ripple across her life in a variety of ways.

Cayetano and Sandra had in fact talked business on the night they met. However, they'd done so with each other. Perhaps it was foolish to think that these weekends would always be an oasis. They each had very full lives, and very full lives could never truly be put on hold. And if she was being honest, she'd have to admit that this was even truer with Cayetano than it was with her, and she knew how full her own life was.

For a moment, she thought about making a few phone calls herself — she'd left some transactions pending — but she rejected the notion. Instead, she called down to room service to order their breakfast and then readied her shower. When she returned to the bedroom after showering, her hair still damp, she found Cayetano sitting on a chair with one leg crossed over the other.

"Not many people can wear terry cloth as magnificently as you do, my love," he said.

"Perhaps I should walk around in this towel for the rest of the day, then."

"You know that would be excruciating to me. All I would be able to think is, *with just one pull . . .*"

She grinned at him. "As though you aren't always thinking about undressing me anyway."

"Yes, a valid point."

She walked over to kiss him, pulling back when his fingers began to wander under her towel.

"Breakfast is on its way."

"I can be quick."

"No, you can't."

Cayetano nodded. "No, I can't. Not with you."

Sandra knew this to be true. None of their interludes over the past fifteen years had ever been rushed, and Sandra had never once felt that Cayetano was more focused on attending to his needs than hers. Even yesterday, when his late afternoon schedule was calling to him, Cayetano had taken the time to make Sandra feel deeply loved. But for how long would that continue to be the case?

"You sounded very intent this morning," she said, sitting on the edge of the bed.

"I didn't wake you, did I?"

"No, not at all. I couldn't even make out what you were saying, but I could get a sense of your tone."

He rolled his eyes. "It appears that I'm incapable of making everyone happy."

"You and everyone else on this planet."

"Yes, but it bothers me more than most, I'm afraid."

She reached out to touch his knee. "You really couldn't afford to get away this weekend, could you?"

"I can always afford my time with you."

"That wasn't really what I was asking."

"I know. And I'll admit that things came up on Thursday that I hadn't anticipated, though you would think I would always anticipate the unanticipated at this point."

"Maybe it is becoming too difficult for us to continue to have these weekends."

He rose then and moved next to her on the bed. "There is nothing difficult about this, my love, even when everything around us is difficult."

She smiled at him softly. "I know you want to believe that."

"I want to believe it, and I do believe it. You're right that it has become harder for me to get away completely; we live in complicated times. But this —" he put his arm around her at that point — "this is essential to my life. If I didn't have this time with you, even though it is not nearly enough, I would be a husk."

Sandra leaned her head against his shoulder. "We're grown-ups now, Cayetano. We need to work with reality at this stage in our lives rather than work against it. You need to know that if I believed that our time together was too difficult for you, I would end it no matter how much you protested."

Cayetano breathed in and out slowly. "I do understand that, which is one of the many reasons why I love you. But it will never come to that. These three days every year get me through all of the others."

He turned her face to his and kissed her deeply. And just as with every other kiss they'd ever shared, Cayetano was fully present, and the depth of his feeling for her flowed through her. Sandra knew that Cayetano meant what he said, even if his intentions at some point might become overshadowed by his responsibilities. For the moment, she chose to live with what they had right here.

When Room Service knocked a few minutes later, they were in no condition to answer the door.

Chapter 8
Castile, March

Alex needed to get physically closer to Ólgar if he was going to learn more about Allie's observations on the prime minister. Allie had confirmed that the aura blanking she'd seen during one Ólgar speech occurred in other public speaking videos as well, but there was still the chance that the medium had something to do with this. As far as Alex knew, Allie was the only person who could read auras online, and that meant that there could be elements of the conversion from live to video that were affecting her readings, or even that Allie herself was contributing to the noise here. She was only ten, after all, and even if she were a prodigy at this, she could be experiencing a learning curve of some kind. Allie swore that she wasn't seeing anything of this sort in any other video she watched or any other photo she accessed, even when Alex convinced her to watch other politicians, but it was impossible to know about the margin for error.

IV had arranged for a meeting with the prime minister under the precept of discussing Alex's company bringing more jobs to Léon. Given Ólgar's hostility toward Alex's business interests in the country during their first meeting, Alex wasn't particularly comfortable with this guise. However, it was the only way either he or the king could conjure to get the three men in the same room together any time in the reasonable future. After all, as far as Ólgar knew, Alex's only function in Léon was as a businessman.

Ólgar was of course late. The prime minister had audaciously asked for the meeting to be held in his offices, and IV nearly acquiesced before Alex talked him out of it. *All* of the king's private meetings were held in the royal palace, and this was not the time to create a precedent. When Ólgar at last blew into the room, his contempt was palpable.

"I told my people to reschedule this for a more convenient time," the prime minister said, "and they were told that moving it was impossible. What could possibly be so pressing as to interrupt critical state business?"

The king put up a hand. "Sorry for the inflexibility, but Alex needs to get back to the United States."

Ólgar glowered at Alex. "Then maybe he should have gone."

So much for standing on ceremony, Alex thought. *I might as well be equally contentious.* "I don't think that would have been in the best interests of Léon, Mr. Prime Minister. Perhaps you haven't been getting the same intelligence that I've been getting from industry leaders, but conservative estimates predict a meaningful decline in jobs provided by foreign companies over the next year. I can help stem that, both by adding jobs and by signaling to others that Léon is open for business."

"And what if I don't want Léon to be open for business to foreign interests?"

"Then you're going to have an even more serious unemployment situation on your hands than you currently have."

Ólgar shrugged as if Alex had just told him that the kitchen was running short on pastries. "I have a plan in place for dealing with unemployment. One that doesn't involve further incursions from outside influences. That was in fact what I was working on this morning before I was pulled out of my office to attend this meeting."

Alex leaned forward in his chair. "With all respect, Mr. Prime Minister, a considerable percentage of Léon's economy — including a huge number of jobs — is tied to the investments companies from other nations have made in the country. If these companies exit, it's impossible for me to imagine that you'd be able to offset the loss with even the most ambitious jobs program."

Ólgar laughed mockingly. "That might be what they teach at MIT, but soon every school of economics in the world will be learning from me in the future. Léon doesn't need Europe or the US. We can make it on our own."

Alex had to remind himself that he wasn't in this room to convince Ólgar to be more amenable to foreign companies. Nor was he here to try to sell the prime minister on a plan that would bring thousands of additional jobs from Alex's own company. Even with his close ties to Léon, Alex was as wary about that sort of investment as every other corporate leader he knew. He wouldn't be making a bigger play here until the political situation stabilized.

It was a good thing he was here for a different purpose, because it was obvious that Ólgar was intransigent. Was it possible that Ólgar could make Léon's economy entirely self-sustaining? No. Alex wasn't sure that any economy could be entirely self-sustaining at this point. Ólgar almost certainly knew that as well. He was sure that the prime minister had a different agenda, one that was going to be far less beneficial to the people of this nation.

Alex and Ólgar had locked eyes after the prime minister's last proclamation. Alex took this opportunity to look at the aura surrounding the man, of course without ever letting him know that his gaze had wandered. What he saw did indeed cause Alex to blink. Because what he saw surrounding Ólgar wasn't the every-color or the no-color Allie had reported from the video, or even the blocked aura that Alex had experienced the last time he was in a room with the man. What he saw now was black. To Alex it was like seeing the devil.

"I'm sorry, Mr. Prime Minister; it appears I have been wasting your time."

For a moment, this appeared to fluster Ólgar. It had probably been a while since anyone had terminated a meeting with him. Even the king seemed to go out of his way to accommodate his underling.

Ólgar's eyes darkened. "Are you telling me that I left important business . . ."

". . . I was planning to discuss important business with you," Alex said. "Now I realize that we both have better things to do."

With that, Alex turned to the king and the two men rose from the table and headed for the door.

◊ ◊ ◊

"It can't have been black," Vidente said when he shared this information with her a short while later. "Maybe a very, very dark brown."

"I can tell the difference between black and brown, Tia Vidente. This was decidedly black."

Vidente took several moments before speaking again. "Do you know how few black auras there are in the world?"

"I know that I have never seen one before, and I've met some genuinely awful people."

"Is it possible he knows you can read him? If he can manipulate his aura, maybe he was doing this to frighten you."

"I have no idea what he knows. That's certainly a possibility. Remember that I couldn't see his aura at all last time. If he was blocking me, then he had to have a reason to block me. And maybe this time I only saw what I did because I'd riled him, and he became too distracted to block me. In that case, then what I saw was his true aura."

"Black."

"Black."

"This must be fixed."

◊ ◊ ◊
St. Tropez, 1998

Alex could feel his PDA taunting him. *A trip to France is not on the agenda*, it was telling him. *You have the meeting with Cantwell in three days for what could be the biggest acquisition you've engineered so far. You should be preparing for that every hour of every day.* At least it drowned out the protests from his checkbook reminding him that last-minute trips to St. Tropez didn't come cheap. While Alex made decent money now, he still wasn't so far removed from his starving-student days that he could easily justify this kind of jolt to his cash flow.

Yet here he was, a couple of thousand dollars poorer and four thousand miles from the massive stack of Cantwell files. And he was here purely on a hunch. During their last night together at the St. Regis, Fernando had tossed off a line about his "favorite getaway," referencing a villa run by the famous Byblos hotel in St. Tropez that offered him complete anonymity to go along with four-star dining and an internationally renowned wine list. If Fernando were going to disappear for a bit of time, it would make sense that he would disappear to a place that had already shown that it could make him invisible, not to mention one that would put all of his expenses on account until he authorized them to charge the palace.

Alex rented a car and made the difficult two-hour drive through the winding mountain roads from the airport in Nice to the Hotel Byblos in St. Tropez. He would not be staying here, having chosen something considerably more modest for his one night in town. Of course, if Fernando were indeed here and wanted to invite him to stay in his suite, Alex had his overnight bag with him.

Alex requested the resort manager and waited a few minutes for the man to arrive.

"I'm a friend of Fernando Trastámara," Alex said when the man shook his hand.

"Then you are a very lucky person."

Alex smiled. "Yes, I am. I need to speak with him about a matter of some urgency. Do you think you could let him know that Alex Soberano is here to see him?"

The man's brows knitted. "I think you might have received some bad information, sir. Prince Fernando is not here."

"Yes, I understand that you've been instructed to say that, and I fully respect this. However, it is extremely important that I speak with the prince about a personal matter. Please give him my message."

The manager shook his head slowly. "I have to say that I'm a little disappointed that Prince Fernando has come to St. Tropez and chosen to stay somewhere else, but if you think he is in this village, I can assure you that he isn't at our hotel or any of our properties."

The man was doing an excellent job of playing his role. A better job than Alex had the patience for at the moment. "Yes, of course. I need to impress upon you that this matter is extremely urgent. You don't need to confirm whether Fernando is here or not; I wouldn't want to get you in trouble. I'm going to take a seat over there. Please let him know that Alex Soberano is in the lobby, and we'll see where things go from there."

The man eyed Alex carefully for several seconds before speaking again. "Sir, I will acknowledge that I am committed to retaining the prince's anonymity when he is staying with us. However, I am under no obligation to do so when he is not. I can tell you in all candor that Fernando Trastámara is not on our premises, nor has he been in several months. You can feel free to wait in the lobby, if you'd like. I'll have some coffee sent over for you. But if you are waiting for the prince, I believe you will be waiting a very long time."

It was impossible for Alex to imagine that the manager was lying. Alex had given him an easy way to maintain his commitment and still convey the message. Clearly, Fernando wasn't here, which meant that his hunch had failed to deliver.

Alex thanked the man for his time and walked to his hotel, feeling increasingly stupid that his skills of deduction had proven to be so inadequate in this instance. He was only in his room a few minutes before he left again to begin visiting the restaurants and bars that the palace's accounting office had identified as places where Fernando had spent money in St. Tropez in the past. None would acknowledge seeing the prince. After that, he visited a few clubs that a journalist friend had identified as hot. The results were the same, though he got a number of invitations to come back with Fernando.

Eventually, he went back to his room and checked in with his office. A call had come from one of the Cantwell people that required his immediate attention. Alex spent a half-hour on the phone with the man, apologizing for the fact that, because he was out of town, he couldn't go to the Cantwell offices to discuss matters in person.

No, Alex thought, as the conversation continued, *I'm on a different continent on pure speculation in search of someone who doesn't want to be found.* He hoped he didn't wind up paying too high a price for doing this.

◊ ◊ ◊

São Paulo, Brazil, 1991

The hike had worn Sandra out. She and Cayetano had been going on long walks as part of their annual weekends together for as long as she could remember. It seemed easier to talk while they were walking, and it really was one of the only times either of them wanted to get out of bed when they were together. The walks usually left Sandra feeling invigorated, but she wasn't feeling that way often these days.

As soon as they got back to their suite, Sandra reclined on the sofa in the sitting room. This was a break from their traditional post-hike protocol, which typically consisted of a shower and then a long, languorous bout of lovemaking.

Sandra was looking forward to both of those things, but she was going to need a few minutes first.

"Is everything okay?" Cayetano said, sitting across from her on the sofa.

"Yes, everything is fine, other than the fact that I'm not twenty-five anymore."

Cayetano reached for her right foot and began massaging. The physical relief surprised Sandra.

"That feels wonderful," she said. When he moved his palm to her arch, Sandra let out a little moan.

"I could see that you weren't walking as vigorously today for most of our hike. Were your feet hurting you?"

"A little."

"And you seem a bit pale as well. Are you not feeling well?"

"I'm fine. I think I might have aged more than a year in the past twelve months."

"Maybe it is I who don't excite you as much anymore."

Sandra pulled her foot back and then moved herself to nestle in Cayetano's arms. "I never want you to think that. With you, I am always at my most alive."

"Then your feet must really hurt you the rest of the year."

Sandra knew that Cayetano was joking with her. At the same time, she knew that by his saying this, he was acknowledging that he'd noticed that she'd been less vital this weekend than he was accustomed to seeing her. She wasn't going to be able to keep the reason from him.

"My feet aren't the problem. I had a little . . . health scare this past spring."

Cayetano pulled himself upward in the sofa, though he made sure to keep her in his arms. "Are you all right?"

"My doctor says that they caught it early and that the procedure took care of everything."

"Procedure. Are we talking about a hysterectomy?"

"We are." She smiled up at him. "So, if you were worried about getting me pregnant in my late forties, that's one less thing to concern you."

He pulled her tighter to him. "When did all of this happen?"

"I hadn't been feeling well for much of the last year. I received the diagnosis in late February and had the procedure in early March. I was worried you were going to notice the scar, but I guess my doctor was right when he told me it would be barely detectible. It of course looks like flashing neon to me."

Cayetano kissed the top of her head and then shifted their bodies so he could look directly at her. "You must have been so scared."

"My doctor was very reassuring."

"Still."

Sandra tipped her head downward slightly. "Yes, I was scared."

"You should have let me know."

"So you could do what? It might have been a little awkward in the hospital if you showed up in the waiting room."

Cayetano did nothing but look into Sandra's eyes for several seconds. Finally, he pulled her closer. "This is what I hate. I should have been there to console you while you were worried and to nurse you back to health afterward. It has been eating at me for such a long time that I'm missing such a big part of your life, but this just drives everything home. On the day you were going through your operation, I was probably having a perfectly pleasant little thought about some tender moment we'd shared – completely unaware that just then you were thinking considerably more dire thoughts." He shook his head slowly. "I should have been there."

"My thoughts of you and my children kept me strong. We'd already made this date by that point, and I kept telling myself that I couldn't miss it. I know that made a difference for me."

"So, the *idea* of me helped you. I could have as easily been an inspiring character in a book. The real me could have helped you in so many ways."

She pulled his hand to her lips and kissed it. "Thank you, Cayetano. I too wish there could have been some way for you to be there with me. The day after the operation, I imagined you bringing me coffee and pestering the doctors for details. You were very insistent. And the week after I got out of the hospital, I went for my first walk since I'd been released. You were my companion the entire time."

"Well, I'm glad my specter performed admirably."

"We haven't been able to share the majority of our lives together, but we've shared enough for me to know just what you would have done or said. That means so, so much to me." She kissed him tenderly. "Let's go shower; I'm sweaty. Then afterward, I need you to make me sweaty again."

"If you're low on energy, we could just hold each other."

"We'll hold each other later. Suddenly I'm feeling spry again."

Chapter 9
Castile, March

About the last thing Alex wanted to do was endure another meeting with Romeo Ólgar, but it was critical if he was going to gain enough insight into the prime minister to recommend a course of action. At least this time, key members from Ólgar's cabinet were going to be there as well, making it less likely that Ólgar would be as confrontational and uncooperative as he'd been during their previous session.

The goal here was simple: study Ólgar's aura from the moment he stepped into the room. Would it shift toward invisibility as he began to address the group, the way Allie said it did on numerous speech videos? Would it be the black that Alex saw the last time they were together? Or did Ólgar have yet another aura to project, a clear sign that he had a level of control over his presence that Alex had never witnessed in anyone before?

Of course, the prime minister was late for the meeting. At this point, it had become something of a joke between Alex and IV, with the two of them even making a friendly wager over how long Ólgar would make the room wait. Alex guessed twenty minutes, while the king suggested that they'd be sitting sipping coffee and making small talk with the ministers of finance and commerce for a half-hour. As it turned out, both estimates were conservative. When the meeting had still not started forty-five minutes past the appointed hour, the king turned to Victor Guia, his chief of staff.

"Perhaps it's time to make a phone call."

"Yes, sir."

What followed were a few minutes of conversation about the weekend's friendly soccer match between the Léon national team and Monaco. Alex figured it was only a matter of time before someone pulled out a phone to show pictures from his child's latest birthday party. This had to be infuriating for the king, though IV was doing an excellent job of keeping his anger hidden. Here was the monarch of the fifteenth largest economy in the world being treated like an underling by a person who, at least technically, reported to him.

The COS returned to the room shaking his head. "It appears that the prime minister will not be attending our meeting this morning."

The king finally allowed his annoyance to surface. "Not attending? His office confirmed it a little more than an hour ago."

"They are very apologetic."

IV's brows furrowed. "I'm sure they were."

Guia tilted his head toward his boss. "I'm fairly certain I know why Prime Minister Ólgar isn't here."

"Well, feel free to share it."

The chief of staff glanced at the others in the room. "Perhaps we should call this meeting to a close first."

The king didn't need a stronger hint. He turned to the ministers and their staffs and said, "Thank you all for coming. I'm sorry we wasted your time this morning. We'll get another meeting on the schedule as soon as possible."

The cabinet members and their attendants began closing laptops and gathering together notepads. As they did, Alex leaned toward the king. "I'll let the two of you have the room."

IV looked at his chief. "Is this anything Alex can't hear?"

"No, Your Majesty. In fact, given what the two of you have been working on, I think it's important that he does hear it."

The others were gone quickly, and the chief of staff again took his place at the table.

"I'm assuming from your expression, Victor," the king said, "that I'm not going to be happy with what you have to say."

"You will definitely not be happy with this, Your Majesty." He took a deep breath and continued. "The prime minister has booked television time for tonight. He's going to make two announcements. The first is that authorities have arrested the journalist Matias Sondar."

Alex felt a chill. "The man who has been publishing that series of scathing editorials about Ólgar?"

"The very same."

The king's face reddened. "Under what charges?"

"They claim that Sondar was attempting to steal state secrets."

"From whom?"

"I don't have that information."

"*For* whom?"

"I'm afraid I don't have that, either."

Alex was nonplussed. "This is a naked attempt to subdue the press. There's little to no chance that Sondar would commit a treasonous act. What comes across clearly in all of his pieces is how much of a patriot he is. By doing this, Ólgar is telling every other journalist out there that his critics will be punished — and punished severely."

"Yes," the chief of staff said, "but, as I mentioned, there are going to be two announcements tonight. The other is about the formation of a state-run news organization to balance the corrupt Léon media."

The king threw the pen he'd been holding onto the table.

"Can he even do something like that without your authorization?" Alex said.

IV glowered. "It appears that Victor and I will be asking that question of our lawyers in a few minutes." He looked downward for several long seconds. "My guess is that Ólgar knows exactly what he can and cannot do. He'll sweep this into some previously granted authority and claim that the palace has already given him the necessary permission. We'll get the courts involved, of course, but, if he's done his homework, we won't be able to get an injunction while we battle it out."

Alex could barely contain himself. "But he's taking over the news."

The chief of staff raised a forefinger. "He isn't technically limiting the freedom of the press by doing this. He's only offering an alternative."

Alex scoffed. "You don't actually believe that, do you?"

"Of course I don't believe it. But that's how he's going to position it."

Alex turned to the king. "People are going to panic. This is all too familiar. That's a similar tactic to what El General did to your grandfather before he sent him on exile to England."

IV shook his head. "You're underestimating Ólgar. He's not going to come off as a dictator here. He's going to position this as an expansion of the public's freedoms. That's why he's announcing it at the same time that he announces the arrest of Sondar. He wants to show that the existing media is working against the people's best interests and that he had to make this move in order to preserve everyone's liberties."

"And the public will buy that?"

The king put a hand on Alex's wrist. "I have a feeling that they will. Ólgar is a brilliant communicator. That's how he won the election in the first place. Some will see through him, but he will get a considerable amount of support for this. And his detractors are likely to be very careful about what they say given what they now know the consequences to be."

"I don't see how this can be happening."

The chief of staff chuckled wryly. "You, as an American, don't see how this can be happening?"

Alex glanced between the other two men in the room. "The two of you are surprisingly calm about this. I'm finding it terrifying."

The king deflated into the back of his chair. "Oh, it is absolutely terrifying."

◊ ◊ ◊

St. Tropez, South of France, 1998

Alex had three options. His flight back was scheduled for 10:23 that morning, which would give him time to get a decent night's sleep before spending the entire next day with the Cantwell files in advance of their meeting the day after that. Another option would have been to have the files sent to his apartment, to delve deeply into them upon his return, stay up as far into the night as he could, then go into the office late after a few hours of sleep for the last-minute meetings with the rest of his firm's team. Then there was the third option: to follow up on the call he received as he got out of the shower this morning.

"You're Alex, yes?" said a man with a heavy French accent when Alex answered.

"Yes, I am."

"You're the one looking for the prince?"

Alex sat on the edge of his hotel bed. "Yes, yes I am."

"You came to my club last night and I told you that I hadn't seen him. My brother owns a restaurant in Saint-Paul de-Vence, and I was talking to him after you left. I mentioned that some guy was looking for Prince Fernando, and he told me he could swear that a person who looked like the prince in disguise was in his restaurant a few days ago."

"Is he sure about this?"

"Well, no, he's not sure about this. He said he *thought* the person looked like the prince. In disguise. It could have been someone else entirely. You seemed pretty desperate when you were here, so I thought this information might be useful to you."

"Thanks. I appreciate it. Saint-Paul de-Vence you said?"

"Yes. Do you know where that is?"

"I do, actually. Fernando took me there once. It's on my way to the Nice airport."

"Then maybe he is there now."

Alex thanked the man again and hung up. Saint-Paul de-Vence was a walled town that felt ancient compared to the vigor of St. Tropez. However, there were beautiful views and many good places to eat, and Fernando seemed to shed his persona as they walked the streets. The day they spent there together had been such an unremarkable one that the memory of it had largely receded for Alex. But maybe that unremarkable-ness was exactly what Fernando was seeking. It made a certain amount of sense.

But did it make sense for Alex to follow up on this tip? Saint-Paul de-Vence was about a two-hour drive from St. Tropez. If he decided to go, there was no possibility he could catch his flight. That meant paying an exorbitant sum for another plane ticket, not to mention the hotel, because he'd never be able to get a flight back today after making this journey. And then there was the much, much bigger cost. Even if he caught the first plane tomorrow morning, his connection went smoothly, and the flight into JFK was not delayed, he would have no time to review the files before meeting with the team – assuming he could get everyone to stay late with him. Going into the Cantwell meeting without being fully prepared would be enormously irresponsible, even if this wasn't his biggest deal to date. Alex had been looking at Cantwell as a career catapult, and his boss had intimated the same. If he failed to land Cantwell, would his career stall out as a consequence?

But if Fernando was less than a two-hour drive away, and if Alex's seeing him might pull the prince out of whatever one calls a "lost weekend" when it extends for weeks, could Alex actually let that opportunity pass?

Alex fully understood that going to Saint-Paul de-Vence was the worst of his options. Yet he had to do it. The king had asked him to do everything possible, and this certainly qualified as that. And it was entirely possible that Fernando was in the midst of doing real damage to himself, considering his proclivities toward excess and the fact that he'd gone completely silent.

Yes, this was the worst option. But, in many ways, it was the only option.

Alex called the hotel's concierge to see about getting a rental car. Then he left a message for his boss, explaining that he would be coming back later than originally planned. His boss wasn't going to like that. After that, he placed another call to the palace to let the king's executive assistant know about this turn of events.

Maybe the king would have a job available for Alex after Alex's firm fired him.

◊ ◊ ◊

London, England, 2001

Sandra hadn't been to London in years, not since her husband had surprised her with an anniversary trip there in the mid-nineties. On the drive to the hotel from Heathrow, she could see that the face of the city was evolving, with bold new construction – some of it surprisingly inconsistent with the surroundings – sprouting everywhere. This city was alive and embracing the new millennium, as opposed to Colina which seemed locked in time by comparison. Maybe she really should move to the United States, as her children had suggested, though Sebastian was unlikely to agree to ever do so. As far as he was concerned, Legado's resistance to change was one of its greatest assets.

Cayetano had come to London for an actual conference – they'd told their spouses they were attending conferences on many occasions during their yearly reunions – and he'd extended his stay into the weekend to be with her. Sandra had gone to England a few days early to do some shopping and to visit some expatriate friends, checking into the hotel where she'd be staying with Cayetano (though registered in a separate room, as was their precaution) half a day ahead of him to get a massage and wait for the man who'd been her lover for thirty-five years.

Sandra found it surprising that she still felt such a stirring inside when she thought about seeing Cayetano. Their interstitial communications had dwindled over the years as their other responsibilities grew, but they still found the time for the occasional letter or less-occasional phone call, all of which provided warmth and sustenance. But their physical meetings were so soul-satisfying that they simultaneously propelled Sandra through the next year and left her with an ever-increasing level of hunger as their next meeting drew near. By the time they saw one another again, Sandra felt as though she had been on a three-day fast. *Maybe we should meet every ten-and-a-half months instead of every year*, she thought and then quickly dismissed the notion. Logistical matters aside, Sandra didn't want to do anything to change the rhythm of what they'd created for fear that this change would be the thing that stole the magic from their union.

And yet when Cayetano arrived, Sandra worried that perhaps something had already come along to take that magic. The conference had agitated him, and it took him much longer to relax than she'd ever seen before. He said he didn't want to tell her too much for fear that his disquiet would dominate him again, but it appeared that a number of meetings had gone in unexpected ways, none of which favored Cayetano. By the time they went to dinner, he'd regained much of his usual glimmer, and their lovemaking that night had all of the tenderness, connection, and attention she'd always reveled in with him. The next morning, though, she awoke to find him sitting in a chair, staring off at the London skyline. It was no longer surprising that he got up first in the morning – Cayetano claimed that sleeplessness visited him almost nightly and that lying awake alone in bed was not an option he could abide — but Sandra usually woke to find him working, or at least reading a newspaper.

"The architecture is discordant," he said when he heard her rustle.

Sandra sat up in bed. "Oh, I don't know. I actually think it's clever. Have you seen the construction going up over there? People are starting to call the building 'the gherkin.'"

"Why does a city with Westminster Abbey need gherkins?"

"As a garnish?"

Normally, Cayetano would have playfully scolded Sandra for such an awful joke, but this time he offered her the tiniest smile and then turned his attention back to the window. Sandra slid out of bed, put on her robe, and joined him at the chair.

"What is it?" she said, touching his shoulder.

He turned to her with a smile that would have been more convincing if his eyes had chosen to participate in it. "Sorry, my love. I don't want anything to compromise our time together. Shall we order breakfast?"

"No, tell me. Did things go that badly this week?"

He beckoned her to join him in the chair, and she sat on his lap and put an arm around him. "It isn't that," he said. "Not that things went well this week, but nothing happened that I can't manage. I'm afraid this is something that has proven far less manageable, and now it is coming to a head."

"What?"

He took one more glance outside and then leaned into her. "My youngest son's tendency toward excess has caught up with him. The day before I left, we had to hospitalize him, and I learned yesterday morning that the treatment has not been going well up to this point."

Cayetano spoke often of his children over the years, but he tended to have much less to say about the youngest than the others. Even when the boy was a child he'd acted rebelliously and in ways that sometimes suggested that he was deliberately attempting to embarrass his parents. Cayetano had admitted previously that his son had been a persistent drug user, but he had never hinted that the situation had the potential to be this bad.

"Do you need to go home to him? If you need to cut things short so you can be by his side, I would . . ."

". . . If I want the treatment to work, then I need to stay as far away from him as possible."

The abruptness of Cayetano's response silenced Sandra, and for several long seconds neither of them spoke.

"I'm sorry, my love. I shouldn't have been so curt with you. As you can see, I'm not at my best when discussing my son. The reality is that I'm likely part of his problem. His doctors have suggested that my expectations for him were too great and that he has been struggling with the pressure of being my offspring."

"He has to know that you love him."

"I'm not entirely sure that he does." Cayetano pulled her a little closer. "I'm not always the man I am with you."

"Don't take undue responsibility for this. You didn't do this to him."

"How do you know?"

Sandra turned him so that their faces were together. "Because I've seen all the way inside of you. Yes, maybe you challenged him more than he could handle, but there's no chance that you did this maliciously. There is no malice in you."

Cayetano leaned back in the chair. "I wish I could believe that."

Sandra stood and pulled him toward her on the bed, laying him down and wrapping him in a protective hug. "I don't only believe it; I know it for fact."

"You are the best person I know, Sandra. I'm so sorry if I'm ruining our time together. This time is so precious to me."

"And me as well, love. Tell me what you need."

"I need you right here, right where you are."

"Then this is where I'll be. There is nothing we need to do today. I'll hold you as long as you want."

"I wish that were really true."

"For the next two days, it is."

Chapter 10
Castile, April

Alex had just returned to his room when the "possession" began. At first, he thought it might be a bad prawn. Then he pondered the possibility that all of his worry over Ólgar was causing him to have something of a fugue moment, which would have been an indication of how much this situation was concerning him, since he'd never had a similar experience during business stress. His stomach roiled, and his neck grew hot, and Alex felt an itching in his brain that was certain to make him insane if it continued. He was about to pound himself on the side of his head — something he'd never once done — when he began to recognize the voice in his head.

"*Bisnieto.*"

It was Vidente, and Alex realized that the disquiet he'd been feeling was caused neither by lunch nor dangerous politicians, but by a long-dead relative crossing whatever it was that she was crossing to get through to him. Vidente had only initiated contact from the other plane one previous time, so Alex knew that she wasn't calling to check up on the family.

"Abuela. You surprised . . ."

". . . I never would have believed it. I have read thousands of auras — maybe even tens of thousands — and I have never seen a black one, though I have heard the rumors. But this Ólgar. I no longer doubt it."

127

Vidente's access to Ólgar's aura had come via a network of connections on this plane and the other that would be nearly impossible to replicate. It required a number of favors, of both the personal and cosmic variety, but it was essential if they were going to determine a way to deal with the man.

Alex knew there were few truly evil people on the planet. There were plenty of people who put their interests above all others, many who were easily tempted to do the wrong thing for the right price, and many others whose souls were so weak that they easily became participants in evil deeds. However, none of these people were evil to the core. Even El General, who had ruled with a brutal iron fist, was said to have believed that his dictatorship was a form of tough love, that his nation needed a firm hand if it was going to emerge from decades of economic stagnation and that he genuinely believed that his rule was an extended heroic act. However, those rare few who owned black auras were genuinely evil, devoid of compassion or even simple regard for their fellows. They knew enough about human nature to wrap their agendas in programs capable of garnering popular support and keeping friction to a minimum, but those programs were a distant second to the agenda.

Though he'd been awaiting Vidente's confirmation, Alex had been wondering at Ólgar's agenda from the moment he first read the prime minister's aura. It was highly unlikely that Ólgar's ambitions were limited to a dictatorship in Léon. Alex loved his adopted country, but it was a moderately sized European nation that had a relatively small role on the world stage. Since Ólgar had chosen politics as the vehicle for his agenda, he would never be willing to stop at dominion over Léon. He would want to extend his power to other places on the continent and maybe even to other continents. Was that even possible given the modest extent of Léon's military power when compared to their neighbors? Not under normal circumstances, Alex knew, but the owner of a black aura would be equipped with ways to change the circumstances. If Ólgar wanted to own Europe, and if he were willing to do anything to get it with no regard to the lives of others, he might in fact be capable of acting before anyone else could move to stop him and therefore do considerably more damage than would be expected from an armed force of Léon's size.

"I've been wracking my mind for a plan, Vidente. This is not my battleground. If we were talking about matters of commerce, I might have a fighting chance. But even the king's best political minds are confounded. And it doesn't help that the people are buying what Ólgar is selling. His approval ratings have risen dramatically. He handled the announcement of a state-run news organization expertly, and the polls love him for it."

"He is a virtuoso, *bisnieto*. I only know of the owners of black auras from legend. Their movements are guided by a force with which most of us are unfamiliar. It appears that Ólgar cultivated the image of a boor and a bully to cause people to underestimate him. He is far more skilled than he appears in public, and I believe we haven't even begun to see his most masterful moves."

"So then how do we battle him?"

"I have a thought, but you might not be comfortable with it."

Alex sighed. "I'm feeling perpetually uncomfortable these days. What's a little more discomfort?"

Vidente paused, and Alex, eyes closed, studied the image of her that he conjured in his head whenever he communicated with her. Alex had seen Vidente physically once — on a cliff side in Southern California on the night that his life made its most profound shift — and he'd seen numerous family photos. He'd settled on a vision of his great-great grandmother in the later stages of her life, even though he was sure that she would have preferred that he imagine a much younger version with smoother skin, since she was nearly as well known for her vanity as she was for her skills at predicting the future.

"Allie has remarkable gifts," she said.

"I agree. She's seeing things in ways that none of us ever have before."

"I think there might be a way for the three of us to work on Ólgar at the same time."

"Work on?"

"Yes. Bathe him in powerful doses of energy all at once: you on the physical plane, me on the aetheric plane, and Allie on the . . . I guess you would call it *digital* plane."

Alex took a moment to register what Vidente was saying. "You want me to have my daughter participate in killing the prime minister of Léon?"

Vidente laughed. "Kill him? We aren't warriors. I was suggesting that we overwhelm him with white light. I have no idea if this will help neutralize someone with a black aura, but it might be our only option."

Alex shook his head, though he was never sure if Vidente could actually see him during these conversations. "I can't put Allie at risk."

"She won't be, unless Ólgar has already taken over the Internet, in which case she's way past the point of being at risk. Allie can do what she needs to do from a safe distance. It's you who will be at the greatest risk. You will need to be in the same room with him, and if he senses you're doing something to him, he will have you removed. And where he sends you after that will be anyone's guess."

Alex allowed himself to think for a moment about Ólgar's security people dragging him out of the room and taking him to some undisclosed location where even the king wouldn't be able to find him. The idea of becoming a political prisoner or laying his life on the line for a cause he believed in was a foreign concept. He couldn't imagine himself going down that way.

He quickly tossed away the image.

"I'm not going to worry about that," he said. "However, we might have a substantial logistical problem. I assume when you say that I need to be in the same room with him, you're not talking about my attending one of his speeches."

"The smaller the room and the fewer others in that room, the better our chances of success."

"That's our problem right there. As I might have mentioned, Ólgar is not a fan of mine. It's unlikely he'll be inviting me to lunch."

"You need to find a way to get a meeting with him."

Alex pondered the possibilities. Stopping a uniquely evil person by triangulating positive light in his direction seemed like a plan that could have real results. Getting on that person's calendar? That seemed like pure fantasy.

◊ ◊ ◊

Saint-Paul de-Vence, Southern France, 1998

As he parked his car in Saint-Paul de-Vence, Alex wondered how likely it was that he'd be able to recognize Fernando if the prince were disguised. He'd read once that babies could recognize their parents even under heavy makeup because of the signals they picked up from their eyes and mannerisms. Did Alex know Fernando that well? Certainly, they'd spent a good deal of time together since they met six years ago in Colina, but how connected were they, really? Did lavish dinners and raucous parties comprise an I'd-know-you-anywhere relationship, or were they simply acquaintances who happened to have a great time when they were together?

This question of course led naturally to the question of how much sense it made for Alex to have extended himself the way he had in search of Fernando. Surely, good-time acquaintances didn't risk their careers for one another. But if their relationship were deeper than that, if they were the "brothers" that each regularly claimed the other to be, wouldn't Fernando have confided in Alex enough to let him know what was going on with his disappearance and maybe even give him a heads-up?

Following this lead had seemed like a good idea back when Alex had gotten the phone call in his room in St. Tropez. Now that he was here, though, Alex realized how easily this could become a fool's errand. Saint-Paul de-Vence was a relatively small town, but it wasn't a village. Alex couldn't simply go from shop to shop and house to house to see if the crown prince of Léon was there. He started at the restaurant where a man who was possibly Fernando in disguise had been spotted. Alex spoke to the owner as he prepared for that evening's service. As Alex feared, the man had virtually nothing to add to what Alex already knew, other than saying that the maybe-prince had a thick beard and John Lennon glasses. This information wasn't particularly helpful, and that was assuming that Fernando wasn't employing a suite of disguises that he swapped out to keep his identity hidden. Alex then stopped into a number of shops to ask if they'd seen a relative newcomer who fit the description the restaurant owner had provided. A few had but couldn't offer much additional information other than a café owner who mentioned that the person Alex had described had shown a particular interest in palmiers when he patronized the shop. Thank goodness Alex spoke French from his days at Lycee Francais in Legado because no one in Saint-Paul de-Vence spoke English or Spanish.

Alex thanked the man and ordered a cappuccino to sip while he pondered his next move. His firm's Cantwell team would be showing up at the office soon, and his boss would arrive at work to receive Alex's message explaining that he wouldn't be in today. Up to this point, Alex had done absolutely nothing impetuous with regard to his job, and he hoped this lobbied in his favor if his actions now caused the Cantwell deal to falter. Alex doubted that it would, because his industry was all about today's results. He was as close to the precipice as he had ever been in his career.

His coffee finished, Alex returned outside with the intention of talking to some residents. He turned onto a side street and stopped a woman who was walking into town. The woman had never seen a man that fit the description Alex offered, but she mentioned that she would be very interested in meeting such a man. Alex smiled at her and continued walking. Just then, a burst of giddy squealing came from his right. Apparently, a school had just let out for recess, and a group of preteens had spilled into the playground to let off excess energy. A woman in her early thirties who Alex took to be their teacher attempted to maintain a modicum of order, though she quickly chuckled and gave up. She moved to a bench to watch her brood, and a man walked out the door to join her there. A bearded man with John Lennon glasses and a baseball cap bearing the Manchester United logo.

In spite of his earlier concerns, Alex recognized Fernando instantly. The way Fernando gestured with his hands gave him away. That and the crease in his forehead that Alex noticed every time he and his friend were together. For a moment, Alex stood fixed to the street before he found his legs and walked onto the school yard.

Fernando was involved in an animated conversation with the teacher, so he didn't seem to notice Alex approaching. As Alex got closer, he took note of how great the prince looked. Alex had been expecting to find Fernando bleary-eyed and ruddy from weeks of nonstop drinking. Instead, the man's complexion was glowing, and he'd lost a few pounds, as though he'd spent the time since his disappearance at a high-end cleansing retreat. If Alex was here to rescue the prince, maybe he'd come to Saint-Paul de-Vence with the wrong objective.

Alex was nearly at the bench when Fernando finally looked in his direction.

The prince sagged momentarily and then he threw back his head and laughed.

"I knew you were a great businessman, Alejandro Soberano, but I had no idea you were also a great detective."

"Well, as it turns out, I might not be able to be both things at once."

Fernando didn't seem to pick up on what Alex was implying, simply laughing again.

"It's good to see you, my friend. Come sit with us. This is Lisette."

Lisette nodded acknowledgment and Alex waved at her. Was this really going to play out as though he'd run into the pair in a restaurant in Manhattan? Just then a child screeched, Lisette shouted "Patrice!" and the teacher rose from the bench to deal with her misbehaving students.

With the spot vacated, Alex sat on the bench and Fernando hugged him close.

"It's good to see you, Alejandro Soberano."

"I'm glad you feel that way, since *seeing you* has become something of an obsession of mine recently."

Fernando leaned back on the bench. "Yes, sorry about our missed dinner date."

"You do realize I didn't make hundreds of phone calls and cross an ocean for the purpose of scolding you about standing me up for dinner, don't you?"

Fernando nodded. "I do. But I feel bad about the dinner thing."

"I'd actually forgotten about dinner. Maybe because of everything that has happened since then, including all of the conversations I've had with your father."

"My father sent you looking for me?"

"Me, your security team, and a good portion of the Léon intelligence community. The fact that I was the one that found you does not speak well of the others, by the way."

Fernando rolled his eyes. "How *did* you find me?"

"I tapped into every resource, replayed every conversation we ever had, and flew to Europe. Ultimately, it came down to a lucky tip."

"And what happens now that you've found me?"

"I convince you to get on the plane that your father will be sending for you as soon as I let him know where you are."

Fernando considered this for a moment. "We could pretend that you didn't find me."

"We could, but that would defeat the purpose of my putting in all of this work to track you down and risking my job in the process. How did you wind up here, anyway?"

Fernando glanced over at Lisette kneeling next to two of her students in what appeared to be an attempt to broker some kind of peace between them. He nodded in that direction and then smiled at Alex.

"I met the head teacher of this school at the education conference I told you about. As you know, I've always had a great deal of fondness for this town – remember the afternoon we spent here? – so when I learned she was from Saint-Paul de-Vence, I queried her about her approach to schooling. It turns out that our interests aligned. That got me thinking."

"But why did you have to disappear in order to act on that conversation?"

Fernando shrugged and then looked off at the playground. "See that boy over there? The one with the orange shirt who thinks he's Zinedine Zidane? He's ten years old and he couldn't begin to comprehend the concept of fractions. I've been working with him every day for the last two weeks, approaching the subject from a kinesthetic perspective, because he obviously has a high level of kinesthetic intelligence. Yesterday afternoon, he came to me with a drawing of a soccer pitch that he'd sectioned off, explaining that if he were going to be the world's greatest soccer player, he needed to dominate in a particular *eighth* of his opponent's penalty area."

Alex found himself warmed by Fernando's enthusiasm. "You got through to him. That's wonderful."

"It is wonderful. There are other stories like that out on this playground right now. And this is just one class. I've been working with several others."

"Are you saying that your plan is to renounce the throne so you can be a teacher in a small French town?"

"Special instructor. I don't have the proper makeup to be a good teacher."

"That wasn't my point."

Fernando sighed. "I know it wasn't. Do you want to know something, though? I feel as though I've affected more lives positively in a few weeks here than I have the entire rest of my adult life."

"Now you're just exaggerating."

"I don't think that I am. I'm an ornament in Léon."

"So, you come here and switch identities. Nice beard, by the way. How'd you get it so thick so quickly?"

"I'm a very virile man. I didn't completely switch my identity. The head teacher of course knows who I am, but she is very discreet. The faculty and the students know me as Leo."

"Just Leo?"

"It seemed enough."

Alex watched the children playing then glanced back at his friend. "There's no way you can sustain this."

"I don't see why you say that. I'm making tremendous progress with these children and there are other schools in town and in the region."

"I mean that there's no way you can sustain a lifestyle this modest. When was the last time you had a sip of Cristal? And what about the tabloids? They're starting to doctor your baby pictures because they don't have anything new to publish."

"The tabloids will have to get by without me."

"Those are words I never thought I'd hear you say." Alex leaned forward. "Okay, let's assume that you really could give up all of the money and attention. What you're doing at this school clearly matters to you. And the head teacher here should be commended for having the vision to let you employ your approach. But the difference between what that head teacher can offer and what you have at your disposal back home is profound. You could revolutionize education in Léon and then export your example all over the world."

Fernando scoffed. "You forget that I've attempted that in the past. As I said, I've already affected more lives here. That isn't likely to change if I go home."

"What you're saying *was* true, but that was before you exhibited a willingness to sacrifice your entire lifestyle for it. Your father will pay attention now."

"You're wrong about that. My father will make some empty gesture. He'll have me appointed to some commission. Maybe he'll even convince the minister of education to involve me in a few meetings. But the king has made it very clear that education is not the domain of the palace, and he is committed to guaranteeing that the palace never oversteps its bounds. He's obsessed with never being mistaken for El General."

For a moment, Alex wondered why anyone would ever want to be king if he didn't get to make the rules, and then he realized that some version of this thought might have been driving Fernando since he was very young. Maybe his friend was right. Maybe it was best to make a difference where you could rather than miss badly at something more grandiose. If Fernando was more himself here — and he really did look clear-eyed and fit — then what right did Alex have to try to drag him back to a place that was less healthy for both his body and soul. The king knew that Alex was going to Saint-Paul de-Vence in search of Fernando, but if Alex told the king that his search had proven fruitless, the king would almost surely take Alex at his word. That would turn this town into something of a bubble for the prince, because the king would be less likely to look where a search had already failed. "Leo" could go on inspiring reluctant students, and if he ever felt like becoming Prince Fernando again, the world would revel in the story.

"My father really has people searching the globe for me?" Fernando said.

"I don't think there's anyone on Antarctica, but much of the rest of the globe, yes."

"I suppose I should be moved by that."

"Your father cares about you more than you think he does."

Fernando's eyes crinkled. "And the media is speculating?"

"Most are assuming it's a lost weekend. One is suggesting a rehab facility. Another that you're brokering peace in East Africa. No suggestion that you've been taken by aliens, which I found refreshing."

"And none so outrageous as to suggest that I'd absconded to a primary school in southeastern France."

"That would just be crazy."

Fernando laughed. Then he quieted and once again looked appreciatively at Lisette, who was now ministering to a child who'd fallen off of a swing. The expression he offered the woman was one that Alex had never seen on the prince's face before.

"You're right," he said. "Much as I love this, I can't sustain it."

"I don't know; maybe I was wrong about that."

"You're not wrong, Alejandro Soberano. We both know that I would ultimately miss the luxury and the spotlight. It's better that I not start something here that I can't finish. I have one more student I'd like to work with this afternoon. After that, we can call my father."

"Are you sure?"

"I haven't been sure about anything since I was a toddler. I'm guessing my disappearance will be enough to make my father give up about Katarina Villar."

"He seems to understand that his matchmaking contributed to your flight."

"So, it wasn't a complete waste. Do you have a few days when we get back to Léon? There's a new club in Castile that I think you're going to love."

Alex looked at his watch. "Sorry, but I need to get on the first available flight back to New York."

"You're not coming back with me? I could really use the buffer. My father loves you, you know."

Alex held up a hand. "It's still remotely possible that I can salvage the biggest deal of my career if I get on the next plane."

Fernando tilted his head to the right. "You put that at risk to find me?"

"I did."

"That's insane."

"My boss probably agrees with you."

Fernando took a deep breath and then exhaled slowly. "My father and I will make it up to you."

Alex shrugged. "Don't worry about it."

Alex just hoped it had all been worth it. Right at this moment, he wasn't entirely sure that retrieving Fernando had been the best thing.

◊ ◊ ◊

Madeira Island, Portugal, 2011

There were some things you just needed to say in person. Sandra had questioned her decision hundreds of times — dozens of times on the flight here alone — but she was convinced she'd made the right one. She could have called, she could have written, these days she could even have texted to the private number that Cayetano had provided her. They'd been in contact numerous times over the past few months making arrangements for this trip. Cayetano had even given her an opening when he noted that she'd been in contact more often recently. But Sandra chose not to say anything. *In person is best*, she told herself once again.

Sandra had never been to Portugal before, though as her business had grown throughout South America, she'd become quite proficient at Portuguese to accommodate her expanding Brazilian clientele. Going to Madeira to meet Cayetano this year had been her idea, since she was craving newness. The stately cliff side resort in Funchal was hardly the definition of "new," but the vistas were new to her, and she spent long hours alternating between the book she was reading and staring out into the endless Atlantic during the time she waited for Cayetano's arrival.

Maybe this was a place for a vacation home. Of course, there were so many choices available in Europe, not to mention those closer to her homeland or the one she was about to adopt. Still, this might be a very good choice. There was something so serene and undramatic here that combined with the sheer natural beauty of the place to make Sandra find a level of equilibrium she hadn't found in several years.

This was all going to change now that Cayetano had arrived, though. He'd left her a message a few minutes ago saying that he'd checked in to his room and would be up to see her shortly. With his arrival imminent, Sandra suddenly wished she'd already told him what she needed to tell him. Then it would be behind them and the weekend could proceed the way they nearly always did. That was the issue with putting off difficult things, of course. At some point, you get to the stage where it would have been ideal to have already faced what you no longer had the choice of avoiding.

Cayetano's purposeful knock came on the door, and a moment later they were in each other's arms. Cayetano leaned back to kiss her, but Sandra held him close, needing him right here and right in this moment for a little while longer. He seemed to understand and rested his head on top of hers, breathing softly, waiting for Sandra to make the next move.

Eventually, she stepped back, kissed him gently, and guided him toward the sofa.

"We've been together for nearly two minutes," he said as they sat, "and both of us are still fully clothed. Please tell me you aren't breaking up with me."

Sandra smiled and took his hand. "I'm not breaking up with you, my love."

"Then I'm very confused about all of our clothing."

The boyish way in which Cayetano said this made Sandra chuckle. He was so easy to love, so naked in his affection for her. Sandra knew that Cayetano wasn't like this with everyone. In some circles, he had the reputation for being a ruthless negotiator. With her, though, everything was out in the open and he seemed completely comfortable displaying his vulnerabilities. It was something Sandra had always appreciated about him, but she appreciated it even more in this moment.

"Our clothing will be gone soon," she said. "But there's something you need to know first."

"You seem so serious, Sandra. Your illness hasn't returned, has it?"

"Nothing like that, no. Thankfully, the doctors delivered on their promises. This has to do with a different form of surgery. One that Sebastian and I have performed on our marriage."

Cayetano's eyes widened. "Your marriage?"

"It has been over for many years now. Sebastian has been immersed in his art, making quite a reputation for himself, in fact. And I have been focused on my business, expanding it the way it demands to be expanded. It took a long time for us to realize that we'd been avoiding being at the dinner table together and, when we were there, we never had anything to say. Or anywhere else, for that matter. I finally told Sebastian that I wanted a divorce, and he didn't try to talk me out of it."

Cayetano's expression suggested that he was having a bit of trouble processing everything Sandra had just said. "When did this happen?"

"A little less than three months ago."

"We've been in contact multiple times since then."

"Yes. But it was important to me that I see you when I tell you."

He touched her cheek gently. "I'm so sorry, my love."

She brushed his hand with her face. "I'm okay."

Cayetano reached for her. She moved to rest her head on his shoulder, but he stopped her before she got there.

"I'm lying," he said.

Sandra peered up at him, their faces inches apart. "What?"

"I'm lying, and I can't lie to you." His eyes brightened before he grinned and took her by the shoulders. "I'm not sorry about this, Sandra. To tell you the truth, I have been wishing for this moment for decades."

Even though Sandra had anticipated a reaction of this sort, she still wasn't as prepared for it as she thought she'd been. Before she could say anything, Cayetano continued.

"I'm sure this has been emotionally draining for you and your family, and I'm of course sorry that you've gone through that. And from what you've told me about Sebastian, he seems like a nice enough fellow and I'm sure this has been an adjustment for him, and I'm sorry for that as well. But, Sandra, what you're telling me is that we can finally be together."

"Or we could if you weren't married."

Cayetano shook his head briskly. "No, that is not a matter at all. You know I never loved my wife. She's a perfectly good person, but our union was always one of convenience."

Sandra did of course know this, which was the primary reason she'd been anxious about having this conversation with Cayetano. She'd guessed he'd react this way and, in the process, put all of the responsibility for keeping things as they needed to be on her.

She took both of his hands. "I too have dreamed of a world in which we could always be together. But we don't live in that world. You know you can't leave your wife. That has never been an option. The fallout would be too damaging."

"Nonsense. I can manage the fallout."

"I realize that you think you can, but you'll be hurt by it more than you think you will. Especially if it comes out that you left her for another woman."

Cayetano waved a hand. "I'll figure it all out. This is our chance, Sandra. What we've had together has carried me through every challenge and every triumph for all of these decades, but I have always wanted more. Now we can have more. I can't let anything get in our way."

Sandra stood and walked toward the window, glancing out on the ocean that extended into the horizon. Right now, she needed to look at anything other than Cayetano's eyes.

"I know what you're saying, my love. Of course I do. And of course I've felt the same things. The day Sebastian moved into his new home, I thought about calling you and telling you about how our world had turned. But our world *hasn't* turned. I can't be a party to the dissolution of your marriage; not when I know what it will cost you. And knowing that I need to be strong for both of us, I've made new plans."

Cayetano moved next to her at the window. "New plans?"

"I'm selling my business and moving to the United States to be with my children and grandchildren. I've already purchased an apartment in one of the tallest residential buildings in the world."

"That's very dramatic. Do you think you'll like living in America?"

"I think I'll like living near my children. And I think I need a change that profound. My business is worth a lot of money, and the Legado economy is as strong as it has ever been. The whole developed world is just recovering from recession and the big multinationals need the booming economy of Legado to increase sales. It is the right time to sell. I'm currently in conversations with three multinational companies, including one from your country. Never in my life did I imagine I would have so much money."

Cayetano grinned at her. "Your mind is a treasure, my love. You should stay in Legado and run for president instead." He put a hand on her shoulder. "Or you could allow me to offer you an even better alternative."

She turned toward him. "We both know that's not realistic. And what I need from you isn't an alternative, my love." She kissed him tenderly. "I need, desperately, for us to be exactly the same. Now you can visit me in the United States and stay with me. But I'm not prepared to be your wife. I love being your lover."

Cayetano's eyes made it clear that he wasn't as convinced as she was. For now, at least, he wasn't pressing it. He returned her kiss and the two of them entered the limitless space that Sandra loved so dearly.

Chapter 11
Castile, April

It had become abundantly clear to Alex that Romeo Ólgar did not feel the slightest bit of intimidation when it came to him. Alex had known within thirty seconds of their first meeting that Ólgar didn't like him, but Alex would have thought that his standing within the financial community, his close connection to the palace, and his holdings in Léon would have given him some level of gravity in Ólgar's eyes. The simple fact was that Alex wielded a certain amount of power in Léon and that staying in his good favor would be sensible for any head of state. Ólgar made it obvious that he didn't see any value in this.

Ólgar's office underscored this point when they repeatedly denied Alex's requests to meet privately with the prime minister to discuss "initiatives that could be of mutual benefit." Alex had expected as much, but he had little option but to keep trying. He'd even reached out to a Chinese friend that Ólgar had made an ally to ask that man to broker a meeting. Nothing came of that, either.

If Ólgar had had even a modicum of interest in Léon's future, he would have done what he could to forge a partnership with Alex, or at least listened to Alex's proposals (though, of course, Alex's proposals were nothing more than a ruse to allow the execution of Vidente's plan). However, Léon's health seemed to be inconsequential to the nation's leader.

Léon was merely Ólgar's platform of the moment. Once he'd taken his agenda to the next level, it wouldn't matter if the local economy stumbled or if the people who put him in power realized they had been duped.

Ten days after the conversation with Vidente that had spurred Alex to try to gain an audience with the prime minister, Alex was in a meeting with the king, his chief of staff, and a handful of other key players to discuss alternatives for trying to stop what was increasingly appearing to be Ólgar's play for dictatorship. The meeting had barely begun when one of IV's assistants entered the conference room with a message for Alex.

"The prime minister's office just called. He wants to see you at the residence at 11:00."

Alex looked at his watch. It was currently 9:43. "Did he say why?"

"He did not, Mr. Soberano. He did however make it clear that if you could not make this meeting that you shouldn't bother contacting his office again."

Alex glanced over at the king.

"Go," IV said. "Of course, go."

For more than two decades, Alex had avoided telling the king about the unique gift he carried with him. IV was so utterly grounded, and Alex was certain the man would look askance at anyone who claimed to be able to read auras or connect with the dead. This had, in fact, been the other risk in orchestrating Vidente's plan: not only was there the very real chance that it wouldn't work, but there was also the very real chance that it would permanently change his relationship with both IV and Fernando.

At it turned out, all it generated was a chuckle from the younger Trastámara and a raised eybrow from the older.

"You genuinely believe you can do this?" the king said.

"I believe we need to take the chance."

"Then you should take it."

That was the end of the conversation.

And this was likely going to be the only opportunity Alex would ever get. Arriving at Ólgar's office by 11:00 wouldn't be a problem at all, and Vidente was literally perpetually available. But they needed Allie if the triangulation was going to work, and it wasn't even five in the morning back home. Alex gathered his things, left the meeting room, and pulled out his cell.

"You're positive this can't hurt her, right?" Angélica said when she picked up.

"If Ólgar can hurt her from this far away, then she was already in trouble."

Angélica groaned. "That doesn't make me feel better."

"She's going to be fine."

"And you?"

"If the guy starts shooting rays out of his eyes, I'll remember to duck."

"That's not funny," Angélica said, though she chuckled nervously. "I still don't understand why this is your fight."

"Vidente thinks it's essential."

"But she can't explain why."

"Can't or won't."

"Another thing that doesn't make me feel better. People who take risks should at least know why they're taking such risks." She sighed. "Don't do anything crazy. I'll go wake up Allie. I love you."

"Love you and miss you."

Alex pocketed his phone and headed for the car that was going to take him to the prime minister's residence. A few minutes later, Allie called him back. They reviewed the plan they'd already put in place: at 6:00 a.m. her time (though Ólgar was likely to keep Alex waiting), she would open as many tabs on her computer as possible that carried Ólgar's presence: videos, transcripts of speeches, press releases, social media feeds, and the results of all the other research she'd been doing in the last week or so. Then she would reach into these pieces all at once, using the method that only Allie had perfected, and flood them all with white light. Alex wasn't sure how Allie's bathing Ólgar's digital footprint with pure positive energy would help neutralize the prime minister in the present, but Vidente was convinced that part of Ólgar's power was that he had insinuated himself into every one of these pieces and that, rather than being part of Ólgar's legacy, they were still a physical part of the man himself. That seemed slightly crazy to Alex, but who was to say what was crazy any longer in this situation.

"How long do I keep going?" Allie said.

"Until you hear from me to stop."

"So, does that mean I get to skip school today?"

Alex laughed, warmed by his daughter's seeing a situation as dire as the one they were currently in as an opportunity to do something as delightfully normal as playing hooky.

"I'm hoping this will be long over by the time you need to leave for school."

"I might be tired, though. You got me up very early."

"Yes, I hadn't considered that. I think maybe that's a decision for you and your mother to make."

"Fair enough. This is very exciting, you know."

"I'm glad you feel that way, baby. Maybe you, Vidente, and I can have a conversation about this later."

"Sounds good. Love you, Dad."

"Love you, too. And remember, if you feel any push-back at all, disengage."

"Got it, Dad. Don't worry."

Don't worry. Not worrying was not even remotely likely when it came to Allie being at any kind of risk. He couldn't even sleep any time Allie spent the night at a friend's house, and he was fairly certain that none of his daughter's friends carried a black aura and had designs on world domination. He was nearly one hundred percent certain that what he'd told Angélica was true and that Ólgar couldn't harm Allie from a distance. But he was only *nearly* one hundred percent certain.

Alex returned the phone to his breast pocket. Then he closed his eyes and reached out to Vidente, making sure that she was ready with her end of the operation. Vidente already knew about the call from Ólgar's office, which prompted Alex to wonder just how much of his day-to-day life his great-grandmother could see. Was a part of her always monitoring him? Surely, she respected his privacy, no? Yet another thing to address at the right time.

The speculation provided a useful diversion as the car drew closer to the prime minister's residence. Alex had been trying to avoid feeling apprehensive about the coming meeting, but now that he'd confirmed that all plans were in place, all he could think about was what was about to happen. He had to believe that the intervention on Ólgar was going to work because it would be foolish to go into this thinking otherwise. At the same time, though, it was a bit like poking a sleeping bear. The prime minister owned a black aura, which made him almost incomprehensively lethal. To this point, he'd been belligerent with Alex, but nothing more aggressive than that. However, if Ólgar knew he was being acted upon, would he lash out in a more direct and more damaging way? Sure, he *probably* wouldn't shoot lasers from his eyes, but what, exactly, could he do?

A few minutes later, the car pulled through the gates of the residence and Alex was ushered past security and toward the prime minister's office. Ólgar's executive assistant greeted Alex and sat him in a conference room – where Alex predictably waited until it was nearly 11:30. As the minutes ticked by, Alex wondered about what Allie was doing. Was she keeping her focus on Ólgar's digital presence? If so, for how long could she keep it up? And if Vidente was right that a piece of the prime minister existed in everything he released online, could Ólgar sense that someone was trying to manipulate that presence?

The door opened and Ólgar blew into the room, quickly shutting the door behind him. He was unaccompanied, which surprised Alex. His impression of the prime minister was that the man liked having a big audience around him at all times. The fact that it was just the two of them was going to make Alex's job somewhat easier, but it also ratcheted up his wariness. Was Ólgar planning to do something that precluded having any witnesses?

Alex rose to shake the prime minister's hand, which Ólgar offered perfunctorily. Alex took a quick reading of his aura as he did so. As was the case the last time the two were in a room together, Alex saw that Ólgar's aura was most definitely black.

"Thank you for agreeing to see me, Mr. Prime Minister."

Ólgar sat at the head of the table. "What are you talking about? I called you here."

Was Ólgar truly unaware that Alex had been requesting a meeting for nearly two weeks? Or was he just toying with him in an attempt to keep Alex unmoored? Alex reminded himself that he was dealing with a world-class manipulator and that he couldn't let anything Ólgar did distract him from his purpose.

"Right, of course," Alex said.

Ólgar looked at him condescendingly. "My people tell me you're a smart guy, Soberano. Maybe my people are wrong about that."

Alex let the swipe pass. It was too blatant to be anything other than a reflection of who the prime minister truly was.

Ólgar leaned toward him. "I don't have a lot of time, so I'm going to get right to the point. I want our airline back."

The demand caught Alex completely by surprise. He hadn't anticipated that the prime minister might have his own agenda for this meeting, and he certainly wouldn't have guessed that any such agenda would include a conversation about the Léon national airline. While Alex's company was the majority stakeholder, the purchase of the airline had been a joint venture among more than a dozen companies for a very simple reason: it was nearly impossible to turn much of a profit. Alex had pulled this deal together as a bailout, because a failure of the airline would have been devastating to Léon's economy. Surely Ólgar knew that the airline was barely breaking even; why would he want to put this burden back on his country?

"I will be happy to take any legitimate offer to the board," Alex said.

Ólgar's eyes darkened. "I'm not interested in what your board has to say. It is not in the best interests of this country to have our national airline under foreign ownership."

Alex was sure that Ólgar knew that the airline wasn't technically owned by foreigners. Several of the companies in the joint venture were Léon based, and the previous prime minister had made Alex a citizen of Léon to guarantee that a majority of the airline's ownership stayed within the national borders.

"While I'm chairman of the board, I can't make any decision of this sort unilaterally."

Ólgar threw up his hands. "That is nonsense. I'm more than a little familiar with what chairmen can and cannot do. If you won't take the initiative on your own, I'll invoke the national security clause."

The prime minister was referring to a clause in the purchase agreement that said that Léon could buy back the airline for a pre-determined price calculation if it was deemed to be crucial to national security.

"The national security clause has specific conditions attached to it. I don't believe most of those conditions have been met."

Ólgar leaned toward Alex and fixed him with his gaze. "You're going to do this, Soberano."

Ólgar had thrown Alex off his game with his surprise agenda. The prime minister's glare, however, gave Alex the opportunity to refocus. There was no way for him to know in this moment if Vidente and Allie were working in concert with him, but Alex needed to act. Using a technique taught to him by a woman who'd died decades before Alex was born,

Alex fixed on Ólgar's black aura and bathed it with pure white light.

"Are you in there, Soberano?"

Alex wasn't sure what he looked like to Ólgar in this moment. Let the prime minister think that he'd so intimidated Alex that Alex had been left speechless. Ólgar's ego would swell from this, and there was an excellent chance that this would allow Alex more time to continue his attack. Still, he had to say something.

"I'm trying to think of a way to make this work," Alex said.

"There's nothing to think about. You can make this easy by agreeing to the deal right now, or I invoke the national security clause and it gets done anyway."

Alex pushed the white light harder. He knew he wasn't going to have much more time. Given Ólgar's power, the prime minister was likely to figure out what Alex was doing soon. And beyond that, he was just as likely to get up from the table and leave the conference room at any moment.

Meanwhile, the prime minister's aura continued to be as black as ever. Alex wished there was a way to know if Vidente and Allie were pushing as hard as he was pushing right now. Vidente's theory was that hitting Ólgar aggressively on three levels at once would neutralize the man's intense negative energies because he wouldn't be prepared to defend himself on all three fronts at the same time. But not only was this nothing more than a theory, there was no way with Alex in the conference room for the three of them to know if they were all using maximum effort concurrently.

Just then, Alex noticed a rumble at the crown of Ólgar's aura, as though something were burrowing up from inside. Then he saw a spume of gray leap like a solar flare from this same spot. Alex thought he heard the tiniest percussion, as though a pressurized cap had been released, but acknowledged that his mind might be adding a soundtrack to this visual. He intensified his efforts, and more gray lifted off in flecks and floated away from the prime minister's aura. And then, with a suddenness that caused air to catch in Alex's throat, the black began leaking from this opening, causing the prime minister's aura to thin noticeably.

Ólgar sagged for a second and then stood, leaning both hands on the conference table. "What are you trying to do to me? You devil! I knew you were one of them from the day I met you."

Subterfuge was unnecessary at this point. Ólgar clearly knew he was under attack. Alex said nothing and pushed white light with every ounce of will he contained. The black continued to leak from the prime minister's aura, and the aura continued to shrink. Where it had been a good two inches around Ólgar when he entered the conference room, now it hugged the man like a thin membrane.

"I knew there was a reason I hated you instantly, Soberano."

Alex's name caught in the prime minister's throat as the prime minister's aura receded completely. Ólgar stumbled forward, his elbows landing on the conference room table with enough force to cause his protection detail to burst into the room. When they arrived, they found their boss slumped back in his chair, sweating profusely, his eyes unfocused.

"What happened here?" one of the men said to Alex while the other attended to Ólgar.

"I'm not sure," Alex said. "One moment he was doing everything he could to try to intimidate me and the next he crashed on the table before falling back in his chair."

Ólgar was incoherent and breathing rapidly. The man attending to him called for medical assistance.

"Mr. Soberano, we're going to have to hold you for questioning while the doctors look at the prime minister."

"I understand."

Alex knew that they would need to clear him of having anything to do with the prime minister's sudden illness. Of course, there would be no signs of a physical attack, and he would be free to go. If Ólgar himself tried to suggest that Alex had accosted him psychically, the doctors would interpret this as a sign that the prime minister's health was still impaired. After all, who believed in psychic attacks? This was assuming, of course, that Ólgar didn't have so much control over his team that they would deny their professional responsibilities in order to benefit him.

It took less than two minutes for the medical team to arrive, at which point the head of Ólgar's security took Alex into another room to debrief him.

"You say the prime minister was especially exercised?"

Alex nodded. "He insisted that I sell him back the national airline, and when I told him that doing so wouldn't be as simple as he wanted it to be, he got increasingly belligerent. And then he collapsed. Do you think it was a heart attack or a stroke?"

"I'm not a doctor, Mr. Soberano. Was there any physical scuffle between the two of you?"

"No, of course not. Don't you have all of this on video? There must be cameras in the conference room."

"The prime minister insisted that we turn them off before he entered the room. It's not the first time he's made this sort of demand."

Alex wondered what the man was implying. Did Ólgar make a habit of using that room to go beyond the law?

"I didn't touch the prime minister."

The security man watched Alex for a moment and then said, "I have no doubt that this is the case, Mr. Soberano. You're still staying at the palace, I assume."

"Yes, I am."

"We'll reach out there if we need to contact you further. I can't imagine that it will be necessary, but please inform us if you intend to return to the United States."

"I understand."

"You're free to leave."

Alex stood and walked toward the door.

"Mr. Soberano?"

Alex turned back toward the man. "Yes?"

"Thank you for your cooperation."

Alex thought this was an odd thing to say under the circumstances, but he didn't say anything more. Instead, he left the residence and got into the car that was waiting for him. Once they were on the road, he pulled out his phone to call his daughter.

"I'm on the way back to the palace, Babe."

"I know. Vidente told me."

"You've been talking to Vidente?"

"She was keeping an eye on you. She told me when it was time to push as hard as I could."

"The three of us definitely need to talk later. Did you discuss the idea of taking the day off with Mom?"

"We've already made lunch plans. I'm gonna go back to bed now."

"You do that. I love you, Babe."

"Love you, too."

When he got off the phone, Alex noticed that the car he was in was stuck in traffic. It was going to be a while before he got back to the palace, and he didn't want to call the king, because he thought it would be better to discuss this in person. Instead, he reached out to his great-grandmother. Doing so had always required Alex to enter a deep place of calm, a meditative state where he erased thought about anything other than Vidente and whatever it was that they were going to discuss. Given everything he'd just experienced, though, calm was highly unlikely. He could only hope that, if he focused hard enough, he'd be able to get through to her. He closed his eyes and fixed his mind on a spot to his upper right. But he'd been doing so for only a few seconds when he felt the burning of his neck and the itching in his brain. Vidente had "dialed his number" first.

"Do you have any idea what happened in there?" he said.

"I believe we sapped his bioelectric energies."

"That wasn't what we were trying to do, was it?"

"We were trying to neutralize the black. When all of us pushed with full force at the same time, we did that. What I hadn't anticipated was that there might actually be nothing other than black in his aura — that all of the other auras he'd been projecting were just illusions."

"So, what happens now?"

"He is very weak."

"Will he get better?"

"It will take some time, but I believe so."

"And when he regains his strength, will his aura be black again?"

"This is the question I can't answer. I suppose we'll have to wait to find out."

Chapter 12
Castile, 1998

"D o you know what I like about you, Alejandro Soberano?" Fernando said.

"That I'm willing to go along with just about any crazy idea for entertainment you might have?"

"I do like that. But I was thinking about something else. I was thinking that I like the fact that you take action. You *do things*, you know?"

Alex found there was a certain amount of irony in this statement. He was back at the palace on the king's invitation because he'd in fact done something, but it was only in response to Fernando uncharacteristically doing something himself. And that he'd been able to get the time to come here at all had been the result of his doing something – closing the Cantwell deal – but only after his inaction on that front had nearly caused the deal to collapse. The meeting the day after he returned from retrieving Fernando had not gone well, because he hadn't been able to orchestrate the pitch with his team as comprehensively as he usually did. If not for an eleventh-hour phone call between Alex and Cantwell's CFO, Alex's ascension at the firm could have come to an abrupt halt and led to his being ushered out the door. Instead, he got some extra comp time for getting Cantwell on board.

He and Fernando were walking through the palace gardens. Fernando was essentially under "house arrest," his father barring him from any globetrotting for at least six months.

"What about you?" Alex said. "Are you taking any action?"

Fernando made a show of looking at everything but Alex, obviously pretending he hadn't heard Alex's question.

"We keep not talking about this, Fernando. What are you doing about your experiences in Saint-Paul de-Vence?"

Fernando gazed up at the sky. "Remembering them fondly."

"You're really not going to take this any further?"

"How would I do that?"

"It sounded to me like you'd made some awfully big breakthroughs in terms of your education initiative while you were there. What are you doing with that?"

"My father is suggesting a symposium. He suggests it nearly every day."

"A symposium sounds like an extremely good idea. You can invite the best minds on education from all around the world. Get other people working on this, and see how far you can take it."

"That sounds like something you would do, Alejandro Soberano, not like something I would do."

Alex stopped walking and turned toward his friend. "This matters to you, doesn't it?"

Fernando offered a slow shrug.

"Fernando, I saw you in France. You were electric. Why wouldn't you want to be like that all the time?"

"First of all, that was very hard. I don't know if you're aware of this, but working is a real labor."

"I've heard."

"And then there's the matter of how everyone is dealing with me on this. My father keeps talking to me about 'my project,' as though it were something I would do to keep myself amused. He did arrange for me to get on the Minister of Education's calendar multiple times. The minister thinks trying something experimental might have applications in a handful of instances. I think he's largely saying this to placate me, but what he's really saying is that my approach to education could never work on a broad scale."

"So, you take baby steps. You make them let you try it out in one school – *one school*. Just like you were doing in Saint-Paul de-Vence. And then when you have measurables, you roll it out to more schools, and then an entire region. Soon enough, all of Léon will be excelling under the Trastámara Method. After that, the rest of the world will be clamoring for your help, which you will happily arrange to provide."

Fernando chuckled. "That doesn't sound remotely in character for me. Have I mentioned that I admire the fact that you take action?"

"You're really not going to go anywhere with this."

"I got what I wanted out of my little adventure. My father has stopped talking about marrying me off, and I was able to pretend I was someone else for a little while, and that someone else helped a few kids."

"So, what's the plan going forward?"

"Well, I'm still stuck here for a little while, but I'm doing my research. After that, though, I'm thinking the Far East. I've heard Singapore's nightlife is a revelation. How about we plan a trip there next spring?"

◊ ◊ ◊

Castile, April

Alex was preparing to head back home at last. Though Ól-gar's media people tried very hard to keep the news of his hospitalization quiet, speculation was all over the Internet within hours, and all of the major news agencies were reporting it as fact by that evening. While much of this had stayed out of the news, doctors indicated that the prime minister's recovery had been extremely slow, with reports of his being prone to incoherent rants before passing into deep sleep for a dozen hours at a time. The hospital had run an endless number of tests on the man trying to determine the cause of his illness, ruling out everything from neurological disorder to heart failure to cancer in the process, though understandably none had thought to examine his personal electromagnetic field. All they could determine for sure was that the prime minister's blood pressure was extremely low and that his cognitive function was somewhat impaired. They still believed that recovery was likely, though no one could say definitively. The conclusion was that he was extremely tired and overworked.

Alex wasn't sure what any of this meant. Had they simply sucker-punched the prime minister with no real long-term ramifications to their actions? Had they permanently drained the blackness from Ólgar's aura? What did it mean that Ólgar's aura had seemed to dissipate completely while Alex was in the conference room with him? Didn't everyone have some kind of aura? And if the man recovered fully, would all of the darkness he carried recover with him?

Now that they were on the other side of it, Alex allowed himself to consider how he would define the optimal outcome. He'd been so focused on getting rid of the black that he hadn't played out the rest of the scenario in his mind. Who would Ólgar be without a black aura? Would he be a reasonable politician who would work with the palace to address Léon's needs? Would he be utterly ineffectual without the darkness, stumbling through the rest of his term and leaving the country a step behind on the world stage? Would the black simply "grow back," making him just as dangerous and far more prepared for any subsequent attack? As was the case with so many conflicts, the need to act was clear, but the consequences of any action were less so.

For the first few days after Ólgar's hospitalization, Alex had continued to meet with the king and others in the palace to discuss next steps, playing out various scenarios depending on how the prime minister rebounded from his medical condition. Of course, only the king, Fernando, and Alex knew what Alex had done to cause Ólgar's infirmity, though none of them had any idea what effect Alex, Vidente, and Allie had truly had and how it would affect the prime minister long term. IV was of course getting regular updates on the prime minister's health, but the doctors remained unable to predict the path of recuperation, though all believed that Ólgar would return to full health at some point.

For now, it was just a matter of waiting. The deputy prime minister, Manuel Aliado, was serving as acting prime minister, and the government was moving forward with every agency and department operating with slightly greater latitude than they'd had when Ólgar was running things. Because of this, there no longer seemed to be any good reason for Alex to stay in Léon, and there were countless reasons for him to get back to New York, something he was reminded about every time he called the office. He would be flying out tomorrow morning.

Alex was in his suite catching up on his email when one of the king's aides called his cell.

"Mr. Soberano, we've received a message from the prime minister. He's requesting a meeting with you."

Alex glanced over at the clock. It was late in the day for a meeting at the residence, and he had no idea what this could be about since he didn't think he had any unfinished business to address.

"Prime Minister Aliado wants to meet tonight? I believe he's aware that I'm going to the airport in the morning to head back to the US."

"Oh, sorry for the confusion, Mr. Soberano. It's Prime Minister Ólgar who wants to meet with you."

Alex's eyes widened. "Ólgar wants to meet with me?"

"Yes, sir. He's asked that we arrange a car to take you to the hospital."

"Did you clear this with the king?"

"We did. He said that it was of course your decision whether you wanted to go or not, but he was not opposed to it."

Alex pondered the possibilities. Had Ólgar regained his strength? Was he now seeking to exact some kind of revenge on Alex? What could he do from a hospital bed? Was Alex walking straight into danger? It would be easy enough to decline the invitation, board a plane tomorrow, and let others deal with whatever reason Ólgar might have for reaching out to Alex. But if Alex were in the same room with the man, he'd be able to provide more information to the king. And the simple fact was that he was far too curious to let this go. He rarely let curiosity get the best of him, but he knew he wasn't going to be able to resist the temptation this time.

"Thank you. I can make myself ready to leave in about a half hour."

Alex clicked off his cell and considered this turn of events. He thought about calling home. This invitation had caused his nerves to prickle, and he felt the need to reach out to let his family know that he loved them. Just in case. Ultimately, he decided against this, since Allie was at school and Angélica might become alarmed if he called her out of the blue solely for this purpose.

They know I love them, he thought. *They'll always have that.*

He reached out to Vidente instead. It took him several minutes to get her because he couldn't clear his mind enough to do so. When, repeatedly, all he saw in front of him was darkness, he wondered again about Ólgar's powers. Had the man figured out some way to cut Alex off from the other plane? But then the face of a wizened, dignified older woman took form and Alex immediately felt better on multiple levels.

"*Abuela*, Ólgar has summoned me."

"I didn't anticipate that."

Vidente said this so softly that Alex had trouble understanding her implications.

"Am I making a mistake by going?"

Vidente took several seconds to answer, and when she did, all she said was, "I don't know."

"You can't read anything?"

"I'm having trouble locating Ólgar. This has been happening since the event with his aura. That could mean many things."

Alex had reached out to his great-grandmother for a modicum of assurance. Clearly, she had none to offer him.

"Be careful, *bisnieto*," she said. "Be prepared for anything."

No, there would be no assurance.

◊ ◊ ◊

When he got to the hospital about an hour later, he saw that an entire corridor had been set aside for Ólgar, with security posted all down the hall and multiple guards at the prime minister's door. Alex wasn't sure how much of this was to protect Ólgar and how much of it was to keep news about his condition to a minimum.

Alex announced himself to the guards and then waited for them to confirm that he was authorized to enter the prime minister's room. When they opened the door for him to enter, he hesitated a few seconds longer, his apprehension ratcheting up now that he'd come to this point. It would have been so easy to say he was too busy with his preparations to head home, but that opportunity had passed.

He stepped through.

Ólgar was sitting up in his bed with a staff person on either side of him. All glanced in Alex's direction when he entered, but Alex barely noticed the others. He focused all of his attention on the prime minister, noting that the man quite definitely looked like he belonged in a hospital. His complexion was ashen, and his shoulders were slumped. The one reminder of the Ólgar who'd confronted Alex in a conference room less than a week earlier was the intensity in his eyes. It reminded Alex of a movie comedy thriller where one of the characters peeked out through the cut-out eyes of a figure in a painting, though this particular vision didn't seem funny to Alex at all. Ólgar's body might appear to be frail, but he was very definitely still in there.

Before he got to the prime minister's bedside, Alex took a quick reading of Ólgar's aura. As had been the case the last time he looked, the aura was barely present, and it was completely lacking in color, though he could see tiny ripples in it. Alex would have liked to explore the ripples further, but he could hardly do so without intense concentration, something that Ólgar was unlikely to afford him.

"Mr. Prime Minister," Alex said, stopping five feet from Ólgar's bed.

The prime minister didn't respond other than to signal to the others to leave the room. He then fixed Alex with a stare but didn't say anything until the door closed behind his aides.

"Undo it," he said in a voice that somehow seemed more menacing than his usual voice because of the effort required to say it.

Regardless of his condition, Ólgar's first move always seemed to be intimidation. Alex had stood up to this in the past because he'd had plenty experience dealing with those who made the mistake of trying to intimidate him, and he wasn't about to let that change now that the prime minister was bedridden.

"I'm afraid you're going to have to be a bit clearer, Ólgar."   .

"I haven't said anything to the doctors because they wouldn't understand, but you and I come from a similar place, don't we Soberano. You did something to me, and I'm demanding that you undo it."

Alex had been wondering how much of their encounter Ólgar had remembered after his collapse. Now it was clear. Still, the man had no real evidence that Alex had done anything.

"I don't know what you think happened when we last saw each other, Mr. Prime Minister, but from where I was sitting, it appeared that you'd had some kind of attack. You might want to consider incorporating more vegetables into your diet."

Ólgar moved forward in his bed, though it took some effort. His eyes gained more fire as he did so.

"I want to know what you did to me."

Alex held Ólgar's glare. As he did, he was able to get a clearer look at the ripples in the man's aura. They seemed like the undulations of a wave, though on an infinitesimal scale, and Alex couldn't determine if this was a sign that the aura was re-growing or if this was just its normal state at this point.

"Stop staring at me!"

Ólgar's proclamation snapped Alex's attention from the prime minister's aura. He glanced away and then back at the man.

"You seem to think that I've attacked you in some way, but I can tell you with all honesty that from our very first meeting, I've sought a productive outcome for us and for the people of Léon."

Ólgar's eyes narrowed. "Do you think I don't know that you tried to impose yourself on me? Remember who you're talking to — and I don't mean my position."

"You're implying that I have some kind of sinister intent, Ólgar. In truth, all I did was try to bathe you in kindness. Are you saying you can't handle someone having good energy in your presence and sharing a bit of that energy with you?"

"Good energy? Do you expect me to believe that?"

"Believe what you will, Ólgar."

"It's *Mr. Prime Minister*. I believe you actively tried to hurt me, something that would land you in prison if I could prove it. Since we both know I'm not going to claim that you attacked me *metaphysically*, I'll have to deal with your punishment another way. But let me make this clear, Soberano: my strength is returning. And I have more tools at my disposal than you have seen. Reverse whatever you did to me now, and the consequences will be less severe for you."

Alex noticed that the ripples around the man's aura were slowing. What did this mean?

"Let me make sure I'm hearing this correctly. You think that I put some kind of curse on you, Ólgar. I mean, *Mr. Prime Minister*. This couldn't be further from the truth."

"You're not going to get the outcome you desire, Soberano."

"I can see you're getting worked up. I'm sure your doctors wouldn't advise that, and I certainly wouldn't want to be the cause of any complications in your recovery. I think I should leave."

"You're not going anywhere until you undo what you did to me."

It dawned on Alex that the prime minister was fishing here. Even though he was in touch with forces most others had failed to tap, he had no idea how Alex had done what he'd done, and he'd called Alex here in the hopes that he could fluster Alex into giving himself away or even scare Alex enough that he'd "cure" Ólgar. Unsure of how much of the prime minister's vitality had actually returned, Alex knew that it was best to absent himself as soon as he could. Continuing this conversation was an unnecessary risk.

"As I said, Mr. Prime Minister, you seem agitated. I'm going to let you rest now."

"Do not leave this room, Soberano. I can have you detained."

"I don't think you can, actually. Goodbye, Ólgar. Get some rest. And think about what I said about more vegetables. Green ones would be especially good for you."

Chapter 13
New York, April

Alex headed back home the next morning, the fire in Ólgar's eyes a vivid memory. If the man did indeed recover fully – and there was no longer a question of who Ólgar would be if his aura returned – Alex was going to face consequences for the flippant way he'd treated their meeting in the hospital. Still, there was nothing he could do about anything related to Ólgar at this point, so he had to let it go.

Instead, he did the best he could to get back to his normal life. At the office, he took meeting after meeting with his personal staff and division heads. Some had shown admirable initiative in dealing with his absence while others made him wonder if re-training or even replacement was going to be necessary. For weeks after his return, he made it a point to take none of the office home with him other than his morning email ritual. He'd spent far too much time away from Angélica and Allie recently, and he was determined to be as present with them as he could. He even trained himself to think about Léon as little as possible while he was home, because he owed it to his wife and daughter to be as free from distractions as he could be.

Of course, that didn't prevent him from regularly calling the king on his way to work and even commiserating with Vidente about what she was perceiving from her viewpoint.

The prognosis for the prime minister was vague, but it was now abundantly clear that, were he to return to office, he would be vindictive and even more committed to his agenda – and to taking down his perceived enemies. And he would also be emboldened by the knowledge that he'd survived the best the king and Alex had to throw at him. He would have every reason to believe he was invincible.

Then Mariana Comisario, an associate of Matias Sondar, the journalist Ólgar had jailed for allegedly attempting to steal state secrets, discovered a photo of the prime minister with El General. A few days later, Comisario discovered that the ties between Ólgar and Léon's late dictator ran deep. She uncovered clear evidence that Ólgar was a protégé of the man who'd kept Léon under his thumb, but Alex wondered if there was something else going on. Maybe Ólgar was in fact the next generation of despot, one who learned at the knee of a dark master but whose black aura would allow him to project his power much more absolutely. That seemed like crazy comic book stuff, but the past months had shown Alex that there was a wide gap between improbable and impossible.

None of this would matter now, though. These revelations chilled a nation that still shuddered at the mention of El General even a generation later. With Ólgar still incapacitated, the acting prime minister and the legislature, with the full backing of the palace, embarked on a complete investigation of the prime minister's history. Within two weeks, they had enough documentation to remove Ólgar from office. When they presented this information to Ólgar, he chose to resign his post, citing his failing health. By all reports, Ólgar was indignant to the end, but he was not belligerent, which Alex saw as a sign that the man didn't have the strength – either physical, psychic, or otherwise – to put up a real fight. Alex could only hope that this would always be the case.

"The thing I don't understand," Alex said to Vidente and Allie when they discussed the news, "is why this didn't come out sooner. Sondar, Comisario, and every other reputable journalist in Léon was looking for a way to discredit Ólgar. How did they miss all of this for so long?"

"Because it wasn't there," Allie said. "They found some of this stuff online, and I am positive it wasn't there. I looked everywhere before we pushed Ólgar for everything I could use, and I didn't find any of it."

Alex knew better than to question the comprehensiveness of his daughter's search. She might only be ten years old, but she understood the Internet at a level that Alex could only begin to comprehend. "But how could that be? You aren't suggesting that this damning evidence against him was fabricated, are you?"

Allie shook her head quickly. "No, not that. Definitely not that. I think Ólgar found a way to keep it invisible."

"I think Allie might be right," Vidente said. "Ólgar was able to gain the support of a lot of people by keeping his true self invisible to them. He had that kind of power. If that's the case, then it follows that he could obscure his history as well. If he was a protégé of El General, then he likely learned all of El General's ugliest tricks. I'm guessing El General had a plan in place to resuscitate his rule through Ólgar. As you know, El General made the reinstatement of the previous monarchy a condition of his stepping down. Maybe he did this because he thought the Trastámara dynasty would be incapable of resisting when Ólgar made his move. It might have even worked if we hadn't intervened. But after that, with his aura diminished, whatever Ólgar was doing to prevent people from discovering who he really was became diminished as well. That's when things that he'd tried to hide became unhidden."

Alex was finding it remarkable that they were having this conversation. He'd become so accustomed to incorporating the metaphysical into his worldview that he operated with a sense of possibility few of his peers shared. That said, he'd never imagined the ability to employ the metaphysical at the kind of scale at which Ólgar operated it. With his own daughter also exhibiting skills he'd never seen before, what did this say about the future?

"Doesn't that mean that Ólgar will be able to re-exert his power at some point?"

"I don't think so," Vidente said. "He continues not to have any aura around him at all, even after all these weeks have passed. Even his ripples have slowed almost to nothing. As long as that is the case, he'll be too weak to do anything other than live out his exile in obscurity. I will of course continue to watch him to be sure that nothing changes."

If Vidente was to be believed, they'd survived this threat. But that didn't mean that equally dire threats weren't possible from other sources. Alex knew that black auras were an extreme rarity, but there had to be more people alive who possessed them. And what was different about this moment in history from all others was the global reach that technology provided. If Ólgar had gone unchecked, he would have found a way to spread his darkness all over the world without ever leaving his residence. Was someone right now planning the same thing in Caracas or Moscow or even Palo Alto?

◊ ◊ ◊

The king called the day after Ólgar's resignation.

"How would you feel about coming back to Léon over the weekend?"

"With all due respect, Your Majesty, I think I'd like to focus on my business and my family for a while. Having helped topple a potential dictator, I feel I've fulfilled my civic duty for the time being."

"No question about it, Alex. But we're going to be announcing a special election on Monday, and I'd like you to be at the press conference. I obviously can't say *how* you were involved, but I would like to acknowledge *that* you were involved. Bring Angélica and Allie. You know they like being here, and your daughter probably had more to do with grounding Ólgar than you did."

"Please never say that to her."

Alex knew that Allie would leap at the opportunity to return to Castile. She found the most inordinate ways to bring up her love of the area's flora and fauna.

"You have a deal," the king said. "As long as you make it here for the press conference on Monday."

"After which you're going to let me get back to my normal life, right?"

The king laughed. "Maybe you need to expand your definition of 'normal.'"

"I'm not sure I have any additional room for expansion."

"You'd be surprised. Oh, by the way, be sure to wear your best suit. There's going to be a little medal ceremony for you."

"I don't want a medal, Your Majesty."

"Oh, come on, Alex. Don't pretend to be modest with me. And this isn't open to discussion. While we can't ever expose *how* you did what you did — and I must admit I'm still a little hazy on the details — I insist on your being acknowledged for your help in keeping Léon on course during a perilous time. We're going to make you a star in your adopted land."

"I've heard that the greatest honors are those that remain unacknowledged."

"No one actually believes that, son."

◊ ◊ ◊

Castile, April

The following Monday, Alex was standing in the wings while acting prime minister Aliado — who had already made clear that he was not interested in being in the role for the long run — announced the special election that would choose Léon's next leader. Angélica had chosen to sit in the back of the auditorium, but Allie was standing right next to him, smiling at office staff and referring to several of them by name. Allie was a poised and composed preteen most of the time, but Alex had rarely seen her this affable around adults. She had the soul of a leader and a next-generation mind. Alex marveled at the possibilities in front of her.

He squeezed her shoulder and she looked up at him.

"I love it here, Dad."

"I would never have guessed. You've never said anything like that before. We're still flying back tomorrow. You've missed enough school recently."

She smirked at him. "Yeah, learning about photosynthesis is way more important than this."

He knew she had a point. Allie had learned so much through this experience that she never could have learned in an elementary school classroom. Alex thought about a friend who had pulled his two children out of middle school to travel the world for an entire year. When they returned, the kids' brains were so supercharged with new perspectives and new approaches to thinking that they tested a full grade ahead of their ages. Maybe a year in Europe with Léon as their home base would provide similar benefit to his daughter. No matter; she was going to her current school on Wednesday. Learning about photosynthesis was important, too.

Alex turned his attention back to the podium. Aliado had completed his prepared remarks and was taking questions from the media. Most of these questions were innocuous. In fact, the majority of the reporters in the room seemed unusually relaxed about the proceedings, as though covering the announcement of a special election was a vacation compared to what they had been covering during the Ólgar administration.

"Mr. Prime Minister, can you tell us about the role that Alex Soberano had in Prime Minister Ólgar's resignation?"

Alex was surprised to hear his name at this press conference. Certainly, he was a minor public figure in Léon because of his business interests and, earlier, because of his occasional mention in the tabloids in relation to Fernando, but he'd given no interviews during all of the work he'd done recently with the king, and he had no reason to believe he'd be singled out here.

"Well, Mr. Soberano is here today," Aliado said. "Alex has important financial holdings in Léon and enjoys a close friendship with the palace. But I'm sure you knew both of those things already."

"Yes, of course. However, it was my understanding that Alex Soberano had in fact been advising the palace recently."

Aliado turned toward Alex, who nodded back at him.

"Alex, would you care to comment?"

Alex was certainly no stranger to the media, but he found himself apprehensive about dealing with a group of political reporters. The business press tended to be fairly tame unless you were on either end of a hostile takeover. He grinned uncomfortably, realizing that most people watching this conference would have never seen his face before. In fact, it was likely that no more than two dozen people in this room – including his wife and daughter – could have identified him by sight prior to this moment. He walked up to the podium and addressed the reporter who'd asked the question.

"I am very lucky to be able to call the royal family my friends," he said as neutrally as possible. "The king was concerned that the international business community was being cautious about the investment climate in Léon, and he asked for my thoughts."

"So, you weren't brought in to take down Romeo Ólgar."

Alex laughed, but he was sure that it came off as a nervous one. "I run a large multinational company. I'm not sure why you'd call in a CEO to take down a prime minister."

"But you had a meeting with Prime Minister Ólgar shortly before he took ill."

For a split second, Alex thought about denying this and then decided that it would only lead to complications. "Yes, that's true. We were discussing Léon's national airline. As you probably know, I head up an investment group that has a majority interest in the airline. I don't believe my financial report of the operating losses of the airline to him was what made him sick, if that's what you're suggesting."

Several people in the room laughed, after which Aliado stepped forward and Alex stepped away from the podium. When he got back to Allie, he rolled his eyes.

"Did I sound like a buffoon?"

His daughter smiled at him. "Nah, I thought you sounded pretty good. Too bad you can't tell them what really happened, huh?"

"I'm fine with that, Babe."

Fifteen minutes later, the press conference was over. While the king and the acting prime minister conferred, Fernando and Luciana approached.

"Alejandro Soberano is now a major media figure," Fernando said broadly.

"I far prefer taking questions from Bloomberg."

"You did great. They'll be all over that bit about your having a meeting with Ólgar just before he kicked. I'm guessing that was news to a lot of the reporters in the room."

"I'm not sure I want to be the target of innuendo for a news cycle."

"Innuendo? They're going to deify you. These people hated that bastard. You're their new champion."

"Because I had a meeting with Ólgar."

"Let them use their imaginations."

Alex took a deep breath. "We're having dinner in the palace tonight, right? Not anywhere else. I think I'd prefer not to be seen in public again until I'm back in New York."

◊ ◊ ◊

Fernando was right about the attention from the press. Every news outlet in the country ran something about Alex in their coverage, and most of it was purely adulatory. The few that ventured to speculate on Alex's intervening with Ólgar chose to do it in such a lightweight way that it was almost as though they were acknowledging the folly of doing so while they did it.

Everyone is exhaling, Alex thought as he read through the reports. *They are just so relieved to have this behind them that they want to close the door on the entire incident.*

It was a good time for him to be getting on a plane back to the US.

Chapter 14
New York, October

As Fernando had predicted, the Léon media treated Alex graciously following the revelation that he'd been with Ólgar not long before the former prime minister's demise, with both of the leading news weeklies doing extensive – and glowing – feature pieces about Alex and his work and not mentioning the meeting with Ólgar at all. One Internet site tried to gain some traction by nicknaming Alex "The Assassin" and throwing around some unsubstantiated speculation, but this was squashed quickly when the lead investigator from Ólgar's protective detail announced that he'd cleared Alex of any suspicion, and the hospital that treated the former prime minister announced that there was no indication of any outside responsibility for Ólgar's illness. In the US, the entire event barely registered at all. Since most Americans had little perspective on Léon's history under dictatorship, and since they were largely focused on an ongoing series of political histrionics at home, Romeo Ólgar had never become the obsession here that he'd become in Europe. The media covered his sudden collapse and the subsequent revelations that led to his resignation, but they moved on from it quickly, with barely a mention of Alex. Even among his friends and associates in the international business community the bemused questioning stopped within a week of the press conference.

What followed were six months of the closest thing to normalcy Alex had experienced since he first heard Romeo Ólgar's name. He'd steered clear of Léon, even declining an invitation to the new prime minister's inauguration, and he focused on his family – Angélica had won acclaim for a piece she'd written about a famed New York chef who'd lost his sense of smell, and Allie had started middle school and was navigating successfully through an accelerated curriculum – and his corporation. Some of his colleagues had risen to the challenge created by his extended absence, but they were more than happy to return him to his seat at the head of the table. The experience had been instructive to Alex, reinforcing his belief that it was time to start looking outside for someone to serve as his second-in-command. No one on the current staff seemed prepared to assume permanent control of the operation, and that presented a level of risk for the company that no top executive should ever find acceptable.

Alex had just gotten Allie off to school and was preparing to leave for the office when his private cell rang with a call from Fernando. Alex had only seen the prince twice since the press conference, both times in New York. Fernando was no doubt going to try to cajole him to come to Castile or perhaps reprise the getaways to Saint-Paul de-Vence that they'd embarked on with some regularity after Alex tracked him there more than two decades ago.

"Listen, I have some news," Fernando said when Alex answered. "And it's not good news."

Alex's mind immediately jumped to Ólgar. Had the former prime minister regained his black aura? Was he coming out of exile to wreak havoc?

"What's going on?"

"It's my father. He learned this morning that he has pancreatic cancer. The doctors didn't even attempt to offer him hope. They're saying he has less than two months."

Alex had been on his way out the door, but he now put down his briefcase and sat on the living room couch.

"He must be devastated."

"He's attempting to be stoic." There was a long pause on the other end, and Alex thought he could hear his friend attempting to gather himself. "But he's failing."

Alex experienced a wave of melancholy he hadn't felt in decades. He'd had great fondness for the king since their very first meeting, but the close work they'd done earlier in the year had deepened their relationship in multiple ways. It wasn't simply the importance of their efforts; it was also the asides over coffee or dinner where they stepped back from their daunting agenda and simply regarded each other as men who talked with varying levels of admiration, wonder, wistfulness, and regret over their homes, their work, and their ambitions. Alex didn't require much imagination to guess what IV was feeling right now.

"And you?" Alex said to his friend.

"I feel like I've been hit by a bus and a train at the same time."

Several seconds of silence followed. Alex knew that it would be best not to interject while Fernando was attempting to express himself.

"The bus was the news about my father's health," the prince said. "As you know, we've had more than our share of disagreement over the years, but of late we've found a certain level of rapport that one might even suggest bordered on love. And he's a wonderful grandfather. I have no idea how Luciana and I are going to tell the children.

"And then there's the train. That would be the reality that, sometime in the coming months, I'm going to become king. I don't suppose dissolving the monarchy is a viable option, right?"

"People might have some trouble with that."

"There's always abdication. The problem with that one, of course, is that my brother is such a screwup that he makes me look responsible. So, he couldn't take the throne. My sister would have been regal, but she's been gone for so long now. That would leave it to my cousin who hasn't stepped foot in Léon in twenty years and I'm fairly certain traffics in blood diamonds."

"I'm assuming that was a joke."

"I might be exaggerating, but only slightly. The absolute truth, though, is that none of the options are appealing – including the first. As you well know, I've grown up my entire life under the cloud of my someday becoming king. In reality, though, I never believed it would happen. I was genuinely convinced that my father would outlive me – I certainly assumed he was healthier than me. Or that the people of Léon would just decide for once and for all that they didn't want a king any longer. I mean, do monarchies make any sense anywhere anymore? Maybe this is why I was never as keen on taking down Ólgar as the two of you. If he'd actually succeeded in annexing all of Europe, no one would be terribly interested in Léon's line of succession at this point, would they? A new dictatorship certainly would have made my life easier."

"Fernando, you're more prepared for this than you realize." Alex remembered Vidente's speculation on El General's role in reinstating the Trastámara family to the throne because it would make it easier for his protégé to ultimately overthrow Léon's government. "Your family is much stronger than many have given them credit for."

"I could be *much* more prepared for this than I realize and still be nowhere near prepared enough. With regard to my becoming king, there are two absolute facts that prevail. One is that I am not equipped to be king. The other is that I absolutely do not want *to be* king."

Alex and Fernando had had versions of this conversation since they'd met. But until this point, they'd been exclusively theoretical. Alex had always assumed that, when faced with the reality that he was about to take the throne, Fernando would simply rise to it. That sort of thing was in the blood, no? Of course, there was still every chance that he'd recalibrate in the coming days. He'd been given so much to absorb at once.

"Don't think about the train right now," Alex said. "Just concentrate on the bus. Let yourself process this. Your father has just received a devastating prognosis. And as complicated as your relationship has been over the years, he has a huge place in your life. You need to begin to contend with that first."

"Are you suggesting that I not think about the fact that I'm about to assume a level of responsibility that I can't possibly handle?"

"I realize that's unrealistic. But if you could back-burner it a bit."

Fernando laughed. "Would you be able to back-burner it?"

Alex considered the question and knew that it was one that he would never have faced. His reaction to all of this would have been so completely different than his friend's. "We're different people, Fernando."

"You don't need to remind me. Listen, I could really use some face-to-face conversation with you right now, and I know my father would appreciate seeing you. When do you think you could come?"

Alex allowed himself a second or two to fret over the order of his life being once again jostled by a call from Léon, but there was never any question that he would go. For both of his loved ones in crisis.

"I'll move some things around and try to get there by this weekend."

◊ ◊ ◊

At dinner that night, Alex listened to Allie tell a story about a girl in her social studies class who claimed to be descended from the Vikings and then Angélica announcing that she'd decided not to do a piece about the new head of the Manhattan Chamber Orchestra because he'd been so demeaning to his assistant. Then his mother, who was here for dinner as she was at least twice a week, spent several minutes recounting a conversation she'd had that day with a former client and declaring, for easily the tenth time that month, that she never should have sold her firm to move to New York. Alex tried to participate in all of these conversations, but he was preoccupied and a little antsy about waiting his turn.

"Listen, I have something I need to let you know," he said when the conversation quieted. "Fernando called me this morning with some bad news about the king."

"Oh, my God," his mother said, even though Alex had yet to mention what the bad news was. There must have been something in his voice, because Angélica put down her fork and Allie's eyes grew misty.

Alex continued. "I wish I could say that it wasn't as bad as what you are all imagining, but I'm afraid it is. The king has pancreatic cancer, and he doesn't have long to live. Fernando said that the doctors told him that it might only be a couple of months."

His mother got up from the table at that point and headed for the bathroom. Alex wondered what was going on with her. She wasn't usually so easily shaken, and she'd only met the king in person once.

Alex saw a single tear roll down his daughter's cheek. "I really like him," she said.

"I know, Babe. He really likes you, too."

Angélica comforted Allie with one hand and reached for him with the other. "Are you okay?"

"I'm sad. And a little stunned. If he was battling something when we were working together in the spring, he wasn't letting on about it at all."

"How is Fernando holding up?"

"He's rattled. Primarily about the prospect of becoming king, but I think he might be using that as a coping device. I'm going to fly over there the day after tomorrow."

"Of course."

Allie sniffled. "Can we come with you?"

"Not this time, Babe. I know the king would love to see you, but right now there's an awful lot going on. You'll get a chance to see him again. I promise."

As a practice, Alex tried to avoid making promises to Allie that he knew he couldn't keep, but he certainly wasn't sure he was going to be able to keep this one. He was aware of how quickly this particular disease claimed its victims, and there was every chance that IV would soon be in too much pain to see visitors. At the same time, Alex knew that it wasn't appropriate for him to impose his family on the palace at this moment. Everyone on the staff had to have been shaken by the news, and the king's family had to contend with so much.

"Have you spoken to the king yet?" Angélica said.

"No. I'm waiting until I get there. I would think a phone call would feel very hollow to him. I also think it would be best if I processed this a bit more before talking to him. The last thing he needs is to worry about comforting someone else, and I've been feeling pretty shaky the entire day."

They returned to eating solemnly. Alex's mother came back to the table a few minutes later, and he could tell that she had been crying. It was so odd that she was taking this news so hard. Before he made the announcement, he had been concerned with how Angélica and Allie were going to deal with it. It hadn't even dawned on him to extend this concern to his mother. She was usually so tough.

"Is everything all right?" he said to her.

She nodded with her eyes toward her plate. "Yes, I'm fine. I guess I'm just finding this talk of mortality upsetting."

That was difficult for Alex to believe. Of late, it seemed that every dinner with his mother included some report on a friend from back home enduring a life-threatening operation of one sort or another. Her reaction here seemed specifically related to Alex's news about IV. Had she been harboring a long-distance crush on the king all of these years the way one might have adulation for a great actor or musician? If Alex had known, he would have made it a point to put his mother in front of the man more often. Regardless, he let her comment pass.

"I think we should go out for ice cream after dinner tonight," he said to everyone. "Did I ever mention how much the king loves ice cream? I've seen him eat *five scoops* at one sitting."

Angélica smiled at him, clearly understanding what he was doing. He wasn't going to let his family be taken down by mourning. They would celebrate the life instead.

Chapter 15
October

Deep into the flight, she still felt bad about jumping on a plane without letting anyone know where she was going. She'd been doing some version of this her entire life, though, hadn't she? Even before the children were born. Even before she acknowledged that she had compartmentalized her passion. She'd made it part of the composition of her personality. It fit neatly with her independence, her resolve, her insistence on defining her own fate.

Still, she had been so rattled by the news that everything caused her to wonder if she were living her life right. She usually spent Thursday afternoons with her granddaughter. She would have to text her when she landed to let her know that the playdate was off this week, that she'd been called away on urgent business. At some point soon, she might even be willing to share what that urgent business was, but that information most certainly would not be part of the text. She would promise her granddaughter that they would do something special together next week, the kind of promise she made regularly and delivered on with the same regularity. But did it really make up for her absences? When people thought of her, did they think about the special moments she shared with those people, or did they see her as someone who would some day fail to keep a promise and just disappear?

Of course, all of this reflection − something she tended to avoid − was a direct response to the news that put her on the plane in the first place. Yes, it was probably a cliché that a reminder of life's impermanence had driven her to consider all of the choices she'd made, and that perturbed her. But that's what they said about clichés, right? That they became clichés because they were so often true − a statement that had in itself become a cliché at this point. But it was certainly the case this time, and she couldn't have avoided feeling reflective right now if she'd employed every bit of her strength.

She'd been so consumed with feeling the impact of the news and with reacting to the reverberations of that impact that she hadn't taken the time until now to think of the most practical matter in front of her: what was she going to say when she saw him? Certainly, there had been time over the decades when she'd wondered about how they might deal with one matter or another, but she couldn't think of a single time when she felt the need to prepare her opening exchange with him. But the circumstances had never been like these before. And what she said to him and what he said in return would be in many ways indelible.

And, yes, she was going to have to let him know. Though she'd occasionally convinced herself otherwise, she'd always believed in her heart that she would tell him at some point. But then that point just kept receding. This was likely the last opportunity, though, so there was no more room for equivocation. Oddly, she felt at peace with this, even though if anything his hearing it now would be more consequential than if he'd heard it five years, ten years, or twenty years earlier.

"Ladies and gentlemen, we will be landing in Castile shortly. At this time, please return your seats to the upright position and . . ."

She tuned out the rest of the announcement. They'd be on the ground soon. She was only hours from seeing him.

◊ ◊ ◊

Castile, October

Alex had seen Fernando in a variety of aspects over the years. If he closed his eyes and simply thought of the man, what he saw was The Tabloid Prince – a supremely confident, consciously handsome, eternally unruffled party boy who knew exactly how much electricity he could generate with his smile. But Alex had witnessed other iterations of Fernando: Saint-Paul de-Vence Fernando, Lost Soul Fernando, Calibrated Husband Fernando, Disaffected Son Fernando. What he'd never seen, however, was Dumbfounded Fernando. Until now.

When Alex got to the car waiting for him at the airport, he found Fernando sitting in the back seat. That seemed like inappropriate protocol for any prince, let alone one who was likely to be king before the new year came in.

Fernando clapped him on the shoulder and then drew him into an embrace. "How was your flight?"

"Uneventful. What are you doing here? Did you think the driver might get lost taking me to the palace?"

"I just had to get out for a while. Maybe a dozen people on the staff know what's going on and they're unendurably morose. Meanwhile, for everyone else, we just need to pretend that it's business as usual. I'm not sure which I find more unnerving."

"How is your father handling things?"

"Marginally stoically. For the first couple of days he spent most of his time trying to make the rest of us feel better. You know, I don't think I completely realized until now just how remarkably strong he is. That's stupid, I realize. He's been carrying an entire nation on his back for decades. But I think I always equated that with something other than strength. Now he's starting to welcome visitors to break the news to them, and I can see that some of these people are leaving him with a sense of peace while others are just making him sad. It's almost like a pre-funeral."

"That can't be easy for any of you. How is your family doing?"

"The kids are taking it hard. Emma never wants to leave her grandfather's side, and she cries relentlessly when the doctors say he needs to be alone to rest or when she can't be present while one of his visitors is there. She keeps saying things to me like, 'I only have so many hours left.'"

Alex guessed that Allie would have a similar reaction if his mother became terminally ill. The two of them were such good playmates.

"That must be heartbreaking," he said. "And you?"

"Stuck firmly in denial."

"It's only been a few days."

"No, I think I'm going to take up residence in denial. I'm finding it quite comfortable, really. I should have moved here when I was a teenager. The accommodations are lovely."

"They aren't long-term accommodations. You'll find yourself being kicked out of denial soon."

"Not if I have anything to say about it," Fernando said sharply. Then his face dropped. "But of course I don't, do I? I don't have a say about anything."

That last line veered close to Petulant Fernando, an aspect Alex knew well. Before Alex could even comment, though, Dumbfounded Fernando returned.

"I've begun taking meetings. Just a few for now, because we're trying to limit the number of people who know how sick my father is, but my debriefing has begun. I do think it's ironic that the king gets to do so little but needs to know so much. Yesterday, I had the defense minister tell me about the status of our surface-to-air missile inventory and then tell me how I was supposed to react to this information, not only in public but *to him*. I'm going to be the nation's best-known marionette."

"Your father has not been a marionette, Fernando."

Fernando sighed. "Maybe it's just me. Maybe they just realize that I'm fully unqualified at anything beyond being a pretty face."

"Well, you do have a pretty face."

Fernando scoffed. "Not for long. Pretending to be a monarch is going to drain every ounce of vitality from me within two years. You watch. I'll be a husk."

Alex would have thought that "pretending to be monarch" would be a best-case scenario for Fernando, since he'd never had designs on actually ruling. Alex chose not to point this out, though, as he was here to comfort his friend, not cajole him.

"I'm certain you're going to be a very good king."

"Based on what evidence?"

"Based on what I know of you as a person. You can communicate. You can inspire. You can use that pretty face of yours — for however long it lasts — to keep people calm in the middle of a crisis. Those are invaluable skills, and they are only some of your skills."

Fernando tipped his head toward the roof of the car for a moment and then stared outward. "You're a very polite man, Alejandro Soberano. And you're a good friend. But you're not going to be able to sell me on this. Think about it: our country was recently attacked from within by a dictator-in-waiting who sought to rule over its people rather than rule for its people. My father knew what to do under those circumstances. Truly, how do you think things would go if something like that happened under my watch?"

Alex knew not to react immediately, because his immediate reaction was that Fernando had a point. In his experience, the prince had always responded to crisis by shrinking from it. While that might have actually worked for him in a few situations, it would be calamitous in the face of a national emergency.

"You will grow into the role," Alex said after a brief pause. "Do you think your father was fully nimble at all of this the day he became king?"

"I do, actually."

Alex waved away the comment. "Maybe he was, maybe he wasn't. Remember that even after all of his years of leadership, he still called on me — a foreigner and a political outsider — when his country was in danger."

"Exactly. He made the right move; he reached out for the best talent. I have no acuity for identifying talent, and I certainly have no history of making the right moves."

"You're making this seem more daunting than it needs to be. Look, I don't have any idea what being a king is like, but if this is at all like any senior executive function, you can't be fully prepared for it until you're already doing the job."

"And sometimes senior executives get fired because it turns out that they *can't* do the job."

Again, Fernando had a point. This conversation wasn't going the way Alex had intended it (of course, he never intended to have it in the car taking him from the airport), and he realized that Fernando had been so deeply immersed in his consternation over his situation that he likely had already constructed a way to parry any assurance Alex might have to offer.

"Take a cabinet position," Fernando said abruptly.

"What?"

"I checked, and you don't need to be a natural-born citizen to hold a cabinet post. You want to help make this transition better for me? Become finance minister. I can pull the strings to make that happen."

Alex laughed and said nothing.

"I'm serious," Fernando said.

"You *think* you're serious. There are dozens of reasons why that would be a terrible idea, including what the current finance minister might have to say about all of this and how it would look when he did."

"I know terrible ideas, Alejandro Soberano. I'm The King of Terrible Ideas — I'll be literally known by that in a few months! This is not a terrible idea. The prime minister agrees with me that you would be a great finance minister and at least you would be close to me."

Alex glanced away from his friend. Fernando was flailing, and his offering Alex a cabinet spot was a clear indication of how little perspective he had."

"Let's take a breather from this," Alex said. "When we get to the palace, I'll get settled in my room. Meanwhile, you can choose one of your most spectacular bottles of wine from your voluminous selection and we can resume this conversation."

Fernando chortled. "Yes, drinking. Now there's a skill at which I am supremely qualified. Maybe instead of making me king they can make me master sommelier."

Chapter 16
October

In her mind's eye, Sandra still thought of Cayetano the way she saw him that first night in Cap D'Antibes. Mid-twenties, tall, seemingly in charge of the room. She could of course access her memory of all of the other times she'd been with Cayetano over the years, including the time she last saw him eight months ago, but those memories always came second. That night in France had been fixed in her brain, assuming the priority position in her backward vision.

She wondered if that would continue to be the case after she saw him this morning. Surely, part of what caused that first image of Cayetano to have such primacy in her mind was his sheer physical dynamism. But Sandra was convinced that the more significant contributor was the huge import of that encounter. It was a meeting that would define and direct her life, one made more powerful by the way it had caught her completely by surprise. There were so many other encounters between them over the years, but not one of them could match the first for its ability to radically change her perceptions of life. But perhaps this one would. This last one.

Sandra took a sip of the coffee they provided while she waited. Everyone she'd met here had been very gracious to her, even as it was clear that they weren't at all sure how she knew their boss. She'd texted him minutes after she heard, and he invited her to come, telling her that he would let his staff know to treat her as a special visitor. He'd obviously done this, because Sandra had had no problem getting to this waiting room. But it was obvious that they didn't know exactly why they were treating her this way. She'd never been here before, and her profile didn't match the man's usual callers.

Sandra allowed herself a small smile as she thought about the discussions she and Cayetano had had about his "family business" during their first few times together. They'd spoken about Cayetano's responsibilities and obligations at such length but in so little detail that she had no idea what he really did. It was only during their third time together that he'd acknowledged what that business was and why it would forever erect boundaries around their relationship. Ironically, it was he and not she who sought to tear down those boundaries as the years went on. Because, even if he refused to, Sandra understood that tearing them down was never realistic. Not if they were to retain the lives they loved, including the love they shared.

The door to the anteroom opened.

"Ms. Soberano, His Majesty can see you now."

For the first time, Sandra felt nervous. Up to this point, she'd been feeling grieved, but she'd otherwise surrendered herself to the process: book a flight, get to the airport, cross an ocean, settle into her hotel room, take the car that had been sent for her to the royal palace. But now the purpose for her trip had taken precedence over the effort made to make that trip, and for a moment moving from her seat had proven more arduous than any task of the past couple of days. Cayetano was waiting in the next room, and once more her life was going to change immeasurably.

Sandra thanked the woman who'd opened the door for her and stepped through the doorway. Like so many of the other rooms she'd seen since she entered the palace, this one was heavily paneled in olivewood with accents in scarlet and gold. Cayetano was seated on a leather sofa dressed in a suit that was surely meant to honor the presence of other visitors he might be greeting that day, since he'd never needed to be that formal with her. Sandra could tell that his face had been subtly made up in a fashion that would suggest to those others that he was closer to his formerly hale self than he would ever be again. Sandra would never be fooled in this way, and she could see in Cayetano's eyes that he was carrying varying levels of pain, confusion, and disquiet. *You can't hide those sorts of things from the people who truly know you,* she thought.

Now that she was in the room, Sandra wasn't sure how to react. The crisply dressed woman who'd let her in moved to stand at the side of the sofa. Three bodyguards, one of whom Sandra thought she recognized, secured various stations. Then of course there was the fact that Cayetano's wife and other members of his family were somewhere in this building, and any one of them could conceivably walk in at any time. While Sandra wanted to devote all of her attention to the man she'd loved for more than five decades, she couldn't keep her eyes from moving toward the rest of those that populated the room.

Cayetano must have noticed her distraction, because he turned to the woman and then his guards and said, "If you could all allow us some privacy, I would appreciate it."

They all left dutifully, Sandra watching them until the door was closed. Then she turned back toward Cayetano and saw something in his eyes this time that she hadn't been able to see before – the ardor he'd expressed from virtually the moment they first met. Now that they were alone, this was what surfaced through all of his other emotions.

She moved quickly to his side. As with everything else, she was unsure of what to do next. If she hugged him, would she cause him pain? If she kissed him the way she had less than a year ago, would the difference in setting cause him discomfort? She took his hand and moved to sit, but he drew her closer, gently touching his lips to hers.

"And you said you would never come to visit me at the palace," he said, his voice fatigued but still capable of teasing.

"I never imagined that you'd resort to something as extreme as this to get me here."

He smiled softly. "Nor did I, my love."

She settled on the sofa, her right knee touching his left. Sandra wanted his arm around her, but she was aware, as she was sure he was, that this would be problematic if anyone chose to enter the room while they were positioned in this way. She was here as a cherished acquaintance, not a loved one. Never as a loved one.

He adjusted himself, emitting a small grimace as he did.

"Are you horribly uncomfortable?" she said. "Should you be laying instead of sitting?"

"Only if you were laying next to me."

"That might cause a bit of a scandal, *King Alfonso the Fourth*."

He chuckled softly. "I've never heard you say my royal name before."

It was true. Even when Cayetano Trastámara first let her know that he would be taking the royal name of Alfonso IV, she'd never uttered that name in his presence. She'd known him as Cayetano and then Prince Cayetano (though she'd only called him that once during a playful exchange of pillow talk) for too long by then. And it certainly wasn't as though he were serving the people of Léon when they were together.

"Do you like the way it sounds on my lips?" she said.

"I like the way everything sounds on your lips — though nothing more than the sound of my lips on your lips."

Sandra had been swimming in morbid thoughts since she learned that Cayetano was gravely ill, but here was one she hadn't managed to consider until now: they'd already made love for the final time. It wasn't as though Sandra was unaware of the inevitability of this; she had become increasingly aware of it as they entered their seventies. Somehow, though, she thought providence might have offered her some way of knowing in advance when the last time would be, so she could absorb every moment of the experience. She allowed herself a second to flash on the last time they'd been in each other's arms. How much had she truly held onto? Would that be enough to sustain her?

"I wish we could make that sound again," she said.

"Were that we could, my love. Sadly, it might hasten my demise."

Sandra touched his hand. "How are you managing emotionally?"

"It varies from moment to moment. When my granddaughter is here telling me stories about her day, I can nearly feel serene. That is, until something she tells me reminds me that I'm not going to see her next birthday."

Sandra ached at the image, imagining a similar reaction to Allie or Christina or Paul. She didn't know how she would endure if she knew that additional moments with her grandchildren were quickly going to become so painfully few.

"I'm so sorry," she said.

He patted her hand. "We're not here to be melancholy, my love. I've never been able to be gloomy for long in your presence, and I'm not about to start doing that now. Tell me something wondrous, my love. Something to make my day glimmer."

Sandra had already resolved to deliver to Cayetano the news she'd been withholding for half a century, but she'd been unsure about how to begin the conversation. Now, though, he had gifted her with an opening.

"I have something dramatic to tell you. Something that hopefully won't kill you on the spot and have the Soberanos forever branded as political assassins."

"I'm not quite that close to death's door, my love. And I have cancer, not a failing heart. You can tell me."

Sandra felt her mouth go dry. She'd imagined the moment on the plane, in the car, and in the waiting room. In truth, she'd imagined it dozens – probably hundreds – of times over the years, though she'd always pushed it away in the past. Now, there was no more time for pushing it away.

She had to let Cayetano know, and there was not likely going to be another opportunity.

"It's about Alex," she said.

He smiled. "Your son is a very good man. He was essential in saving Léon from the clutches of a dictator, even if I'm still not *entirely* sure how he did so."

"He is. He gets his sharp intellect, his well-organized mind, and his ambition from me." She paused and took a breath. "And he gets his compassion and his vision from his father."

Cayetano tilted his head. "You've spoken of your ex-husband's compassion in the past. He always sounded like someone who carefully considered the feelings of others. But vision? It seems to me that one of the things that frustrated you about Sebastian was that his thinking tended to be rather small."

"Yes, Sebastian always thought small." She locked eyes with Cayetano and held his gaze gently. "But Alex's father never did."

Cayetano's face flushed, and his words came slowly. "What are you saying, my love?"

"Something that I've wondered if you've always known, at least on a subconscious level."

Sandra expected a strong reaction of some sort to what she was saying now. No, she hadn't actually imagined Cayetano clutching his chest and gasping his last breath, but she anticipated an expression of surprise, a volley of questions, a check of her certainty. Instead, Cayetano looked to the ceiling, chuckled softly, and then looked back at her.

"We had a child together."

"A wonderful child. The kind of child parents dream of having."

"I myself have dreamed of having a son like Alex. That my other sons probably know this is one of the regrets I need to deal with before I pass." He seemed lost in that thought for several seconds. Then he chuckled quietly. "Alex has my eyes. And my chin."

"My father's hairline, fortunately."

Cayetano's eyes brightened at her playful jab. "Hey, I'm going to die with *some* hair. Not all men can say that."

Sandra reached for and squeezed Cayetano's hand. Teasing him was a warm reminder of their other days together, but this wasn't a moment for teasing. "There were so many times I wanted to tell you, to allow you to have a relationship with him. But then fate allowed it to happen anyway, and I couldn't have been happier when the two of you became friends. I knew if you were aware that Alex was your own child that you would want to acknowledge him publicly, and that would have caused you all kinds of heartache. I hope you don't hate me for making this decision for us."

Cayetano seemed to consider the possibility briefly, which left Sandra wondering if this visit was going to veer into something much more disquieting than she'd hoped.

A gentle smile from him assuaged her concerns. "I'm constitutionally incapable of hating you, my love. Some little piece of me — even a conscious piece — always had the thought that Alex might be mine. There are those resemblances, after all, not to mention his resemblance to Fernando. And, of course, he was born close enough to our night in Milan that I would have been foolish to not consider the possibility. But you're right; I could not have known for certain that he was my son without acknowledging him, and that would have changed all three of our lives overwhelmingly. And he probably benefited from not having me as a father. As you know, I haven't been wildly successful in that regard. He grew up the right way, Sandra. You have given him the greatest gift."

Something told Sandra that Cayetano would have been a very different parent if he'd had a son like Alex — and a co-parent like herself navigating raising a child together. But there was no point in speculating on this with him.

"How long has Alex known?" Cayetano said.

"He doesn't know. I would not have told him without telling you first. Maybe if I hadn't been able to see you now I might have said something to him."

"Then it is fortunate that he is also at the palace. I saw him yesterday. We can tell him together."

Sandra nodded her assent slowly. She'd anticipated this possibility among the dozens of scenarios she'd played out in her mind. She'd played this particular one in her mind regularly, knowing that it could come to pass and that she would need to get through it with a minimum of tears. Tears were for later, and they were probably best shed in private. If she were going to do a true service to the two men she loved more than any others in the world, she would need to be strong for them.

"Yes, we will do that," she said. "But can we have a little more time alone together first? I'm not ready to let you go just yet."

"If it were up to me, my love, you would never let me go."

"We've had so much together."

"And so much more we could have shared."

Once more, she squeezed his hand. "I will take great comfort in what we did share. You were my one romantic love, Cayetano."

"And you were mine. The one thing in my life that remained perfect from beginning to end."

◊ ◊ ◊

Castile, October

Alex was surprised to be summoned to the king's office suite. They'd already seen each other once since Alex returned to Léon, and they had some more time in the books for the late afternoon. Alex had been spending most of his hours with Fernando, allowing the reluctant heir apparent to use him as a sounding board as much as he could. They were about to continue this process when Alex got the call.

Usually, he waited several minutes in the king's anteroom whenever they met in these offices. Alex wasn't particularly fond of waiting for any meeting, but he'd always sat patiently here. Being delayed by another CEO might be annoying, but when a reigning monarch did it, you understood. This time, though, IV's executive assistant rose as soon as she saw Alex and opened the door for him immediately.

Alex was still reacting to this mild surprise when he encountered one on an entirely different scale: the vision of his mother sitting on the sofa next to the king. The last time he'd seen Mamá, she had been acting oddly at dinner the night he'd told the family about IV's illness. He thought she'd taken the news surprisingly hard, and he couldn't understand why. That mystery was now solved, though there were several more that immediately took its place.

Trying to keep his composure while his mind swam, Alex turned to the king and said, "You remember my mother, don't you, Your Majesty?"

IV chuckled softly while Alex's mother reached a hand toward him.

"Come sit with us," Mamá said. "I'm sure this is all disorienting to you, but we have something to tell you."

Alex sat on a chair opposite the two of them, unsure of where to place his eyes. Did he look at his friend King Alfonso IV, who fit naturally in this setting with one significant exception? Or did he look at that exception, a person he'd believed he'd known as well as you could know another person? With a quick glance down, he noticed that their hands were touching. More than that, really. They were holding hands. On the flight over, Alex had considered the possibility that he might gain access to a Trastámara family secret or two during his stay; deathbed conversations tended to be particularly revealing. He even mused on a few of them, ranging from a different story about the death of the king's daughter to the connection between IV's predecessors and El General. Not in any of his musings did his mother come up. Why on Earth would she have?

When the king started speaking, Alex tilted his head in that direction.

"Alex, as we discussed yesterday, when one is facing the end of his life, one seeks as much closure as possible."

"I thought we were talking about matters of state, sir."

"So did I. Mostly, at least."

Alex saw the king squeeze his mother's hand the way one did when a couple had an established line of unspoken communication, causing Alex's sense of freefall to heighten.

"I also knew I would be seeing Sandra, and I knew we had something that we needed to share with you, and I assumed Sandra and I were going to spend some time this morning deciding how to do that."

Alex was still trying to get his bearings. This meeting was rivaling the time he met Vidente on that cliff in Southern California for sheer inconceivability. He would never have guessed that either of the people sitting in front of him would have had an affair with anyone, let alone with each other.

"How long have you been doing this?" he said.

Mamá leaned toward him. "Longer than you have been alive, darling."

Alex's eyes widened. "So, I didn't introduce the two of you ten years ago at the dedication in Legado."

Mamá shook her head. "No, son; that required quite a bit of play-acting. Cayetano and I first met in France in the sixties."

Cayetano? Alex knew that the king's given name was Cayetano, but he'd never heard anyone use it before. Even the queen referred to her husband as "Alfonso."

"I'm sure you've already guessed that our relationship went beyond friendship," IV said.

Alex laughed nervously. "Yes, I used my incredibly astute powers of deduction to determine that." He shifted his eyes to the middle distance. "How could I not have known about this after all this time?"

Alex had always felt close to his mother. Even after he moved from Legado to the United States in order to go to college, they spoke regularly. And he'd developed such a strong connection to the king over the years, first through Fernando, and then entirely on its own terms. How was it possible that these two people had been intimately involved for longer than he was alive without Alex having the slightest inclination of this? Wasn't reading people his thing? When did they even get the chance to see each other?

"We were very careful about our relationship," his mother said.

"And my bodyguards have always been able to keep a secret," IV said. "Though let me assure you that they only needed to keep this kind of secret in this one circumstance."

Alex had become friendly with several of the palace bodyguards over the years. Had some of them been the same that had kept this affair under wraps? For some reason, that particular betrayal stung a bit, though he knew that it wasn't in fact a betrayal at all. They were doing their jobs, and they were being loyal to a man they respected and admired.

"I'll answer as many questions as you want me to answer later," Mamá said. "But there's more for you to know. And this much Cayetano only learned this morning."

Alex felt his skin prickle. If there was a secret to be revealed that was bigger than the secret of the relationship between these two people, there were only so many options available. This was going to be one of those moments he'd remember the rest of his life, wasn't it?

"I don't suppose I could get a glass — make that a bottle — of Port before we go on."

Mamá again reached out to him. "I know you're in shock at the moment, and I wish there were some way to make this easier on you. Trust me that I weighed so many options over the years, but I believed all of them would have hurt you in some way. You had a father who loved you. He and I created a good home together, even though you know our marriage wasn't everything it might have been. And then when you became friends with Fernando entirely on your own — though I will admit to encouraging my cousin Javier to include you in the prince's travel party for the hospital dedication in Anhelo — and then you and Cayetano became close, the negatives of letting you know outweighed the positives of your knowing."

Alex took a moment to absorb his mother's logic. "That's a hell of a justification, Mamá."

"I'm not saying I did the right thing. I'm just saying that there was no *clearly* right thing. Everything was gray."

There was no more question about why they'd called him here. Alex looked over at IV, who had been surprisingly quiet. The king appeared to have entire paragraphs lodged in his throat. Had Mamá said that she'd only told IV about this a short while ago?

"Am I supposed to call you Dad now? Padre? *King* Padre?"

The king smiled at him weakly. "I've rather enjoyed your calling me 'Four.'"

A particular irony leapt to Alex's mind. "Well, now I'm four as well, no? Your fourth child. Assuming there aren't others, of course."

Alex had allowed more anger into that last sentence than he'd intended, and he could tell from the way it registered on the king that the man had taken the blow.

"Alex, there's a great deal for all of us to process in the short time I have left, and I fully appreciate how upsetting this must be for you. There's something I need to be entirely clear about, though. Your mother and I fell in love as soon as we met. At least, I did; it might have taken her a little bit longer."

The king smiled over at his mother with an expression he'd seen on few men in his time. Then he turned back to Alex.

"Marriage between us would have been impossible back then, though the world is a different place now. But she held my heart from that moment. So, no, there are no children other than those you already know about. I care deeply for my wife, but your mother is the only woman I have ever truly loved."

Alex wasn't any better prepared to hear this than he had been for the rest of it. He'd come to Léon for two very specific reasons: to spend time with a terminally ill man he'd come to love and to offer consolation and advice to that man's son, who also happened to be one of his closest friends. None of this was supposed to be about him. He anticipated that the time here would be bittersweet and a bit reflective. He never expected these days in Léon to shift the fundamentals of his life. Not since he'd encountered the apparition of his great-great grandmother had Alex felt himself so completely swept from one place in his personal universe to another.

The king had more to say. "Your mother and I have discussed this, and I want to talk about it with you and the rest of my family before I do anything, but it is my intention to go public with this information. I want you to be fully recognized as my son."

Up to this point, Alex had been so caught up in the revelation of his parentage that he hadn't done the rest of the math. Now it completely registered. Alex was older than Fernando. Which made him the king's first son, something that the king had just announced his willingness to profess to the world. That meant that, not only was he suddenly a prince — something he'd barely had a second to consider — but he was also suddenly the heir apparent to the throne of one of the largest economies on the planet.

"A great deal will happen if you do that," Alex said.

IV nodded. "I'm aware of that. That's why it is important for us to discuss everything."

Alex made himself wait a few seconds before responding. "I'm going to need to table that discussion. I need a little bit of time to think everything through." He paused to try to collect his thoughts. "Talk to your wife and children. They should of course have a say in this. Meanwhile, I need to talk to Angélica. We all need to figure out what all of this means."

"Of course," the king said.

Alex was about to absent himself from this conversation, when he found that he wasn't quite ready to do so. "Have you given even a moment of thought about me and what the consequences are for me and my family? I've worked incredibly hard for the life that I've made – and I love that life."

The king tipped his head slowly in Alex's direction. "I know this, and I have nothing but the greatest respect for you because of that. But consider something else, Alex: you are more prepared than any crown prince in the world. None of them can approximate your level of experience in terms of leadership, negotiating skill, and crisis management." He paused and locked eyes with Alex. "None of them have been instrumental in removing a despot before he could cause widespread devastation."

Alex wasn't ready to hear this, at least not yet. His success had been in the corporate world, and there was ample evidence that the transition from corporate leadership to government leadership was problematic at best. And as far as taking down Ólgar was concerned, yes, he played an important role, but no more important than several others. If they were going to follow that logic, why not make Allie queen? Or even Vidente? She could become the first trans-dimensional ruler of Europe.

Alex stood, happy to discover that his legs would indeed hold him.

"We can continue this conversation once I've had a chance to absorb it."

The king nodded. "I look forward to that."

Alex turned to his mother.

"Mamá, are you staying."

"For a few more minutes, yes. Maybe we could have lunch this afternoon."

"As long as lunch includes multiple glasses of Port."

"I'm sure that can be arranged, darling."

Chapter 17
Castile, October

Alex had declined Sandra's offer to have them fly back to New York together. It was difficult to blame him. She was quite possibly the last person he wanted to sit next to for eight hours right now. He didn't seem angry with her. In fact, over lunch a couple of days ago, he'd quizzed her on her relationship with Cayetano with seemingly genuine interest and little judgment, even appearing to enjoy it when she shared with him the level of her love for the king. However, in that conversation and the others that followed, it was clear that he'd only begun to wrestle with the implications of this revelation. And it was equally clear that he had no interest in having her help him wrestle with those implications.

Cayetano's conversation with his wife and oldest (well, second-oldest) son had gone about as he'd expected. His wife had at first seemed stricken, but quickly grew philosophical, perhaps allowing for Cayetano's physical condition, or perhaps allowing for an acknowledgment she'd made long before about the nature of their relationship. "Ours was always an elaborate business arrangement, really, wasn't it?" she'd said to him. Cayetano told Sandra that he tried to protest, swearing a depth of affection he genuinely felt for his wife, but he understood the futility of protesting too strenuously.

Cayetano's conversation with Fernando centered more on Alex than it did on the affair that had produced Alex. Cayetano seemed to believe that Fernando was genuinely happy to discover that Alex was his brother, having treated him as such for more than a couple of decades. Cayetano kept trying to bring the conversation around to the betrayal of his marriage vows, even though his relationship with Sandra (and in fact his fatherhood of Alex) preceded his marriage, but Fernando didn't appear to be interested in discussing that. Perhaps Fernando just assumed that infidelity was part of the package when you were royalty. That would seem to be a fitting sentiment for a man who'd mellowed in recent years but had never entirely shaken his reputation as a tireless pleasure seeker.

Cayetano's youngest son was once again in rehab, having gone on a destructive binge right after hearing that his father was terminally ill. For now, Cayetano had decided not to let the man know that he had another brother for fear that such an announcement would undo any progress his latest treatment had made, though he vowed to do so before he passed.

As much as she wanted to stay by Cayetano's side, Sandra no longer felt that she could continue to spend time in the palace. None of the staff other than a couple of the guards knew of her romantic relationship with their king, but those who resided there did, and that made her being with the only man she'd ever loved feel wrong for the first time in her life. So, two days after they'd presented the news to Alex, Sandra visited Cayetano for the last time. As usual, Cayetano's bodyguards were positioned around the room. But this time, as soon as she entered, the guards took their leave. As he passed her on his way to the door, Sandra stopped the guard she'd recognized earlier and, surprising even herself, drew him into an embrace.

"Thank you for everything," she said.

The man's stoic expression softened. "I take a great deal of pride in my job, Ms. Soberano."

Sandra shook her head softly. "It's more than that."

The man dropped his eyes and then took a quick glance back at his king. "I would do anything for him. And I've always known how much he loves you. That means I would do anything for you as well."

Before Sandra could respond, the guard stepped into the hallway, shutting the door behind him. Now that she was alone with Cayetano, she smiled through the tears she was forcing herself to contain.

"Please tell me you don't need to leave," he said to her in French. Hearing the very first words Cayetano had ever spoken to her nearly caused her knees to buckle. She had always been able to share every emotion with this man, but now she found it important to prevent him from seeing how shaken she was.

"This time, I'm afraid I must," she said softly, also in French.

Cayetano switched back to Spanish. "I liked your original answer more."

She moved next to him and took his hand. "Yes, me too. There was so much promise in that first conversation, wasn't there?"

"Promise, curiosity . . . and more than a little bit of lust, if I'm being honest."

Sandra smiled softly. "I was hoping you were lusting for me, because I was surely lusting for you."

"If not for your chaperone . . .."

"Well, not only the chaperone, but she was one of the impediments."

Cayetano's eyes lost their focus for a moment, and she imagined him drifting back to that first night in Cap D'Antibes. Maybe to the kiss they shared outside her hotel room door the next night.

"We fulfilled a great deal of that promise, didn't we, my love?" he said.

Sandra squeezed his hand. "More than most and as much as we could."

Sandra wondered if this were entirely true. Had they realized as much of the promise of that first meeting as they could have? If her uncle hadn't arranged for her marriage to Sebastian, might there have been a different future for her and Cayetano? If she'd remained single, might they have found a way to upend the conventions of Léon? Back then, Cayetano was royalty, but he was *exiled* royalty with no clear path to the throne. In the face of an oppressive dictatorship, the people of Cayetano's nation might not have given any thought to a prince marrying a foreigner outside of his station, having much more fundamental concerns at the time. If they'd made their love known to the world back then and even married, by the time Cayetano was coronated in the mid-seventies, Sandra would have had time to work her way into the hearts of the people.

Such speculation was pointless, though. Her uncle *had* arranged for her marriage, and Cayetano's family operated from their exile as though the monarchy was still in place. And if she had not married, she would not have had her children, of whom she was so proud, and they would not have had the grandchildren that had provided her with so much joy. And if she had become part of Léon's royal family, she never would have built the business that had come to enrich her at least as much as any personal fulfillment.

What she and Cayetano had, then, was perhaps the most fruitful evocation of the promise they'd generated that first night.

"When is your flight?" Cayetano said.

"Your executive assistant has arranged for a car to come for me in a half-hour. Do you think your staff will regret how solicitous they've been to me once they discover who I am? Are they going to hate me?"

He squeezed her hand. "When they learn what you mean to me, they'll wish they had been even more solicitous, my love. And they will all wish that they'd had more time to spend with you."

"I hope so," Sandra said, surprised by how much she meant that.

The conversation fell quiet at that point. With no one else in the room, Sandra felt less apprehensive about being with the king in his palace, so she leaned toward Cayetano and rested her head on his shoulder. He pulled her closer to him and they stayed that way for several minutes.

"Is there no way I can get you to stay longer?" he said.

"It's not fair for me to do that to your family."

He sighed. "You're right, of course. But these few hours have been an oasis for me."

She rose herself up on the sofa and tilted his chin upward. Then she kissed him with all the tenderness of their first kiss.

"We will see each other again," she said, echoing the words he'd said to her that night in Cap D'Antibes.

"If not in this world, then the next. I'll find a wonderful place for our next rendezvous."

She kissed him once more and then stood. Before she could regret leaving, she gave his hand one last squeeze and then moved toward the door.

◊ ◊ ◊

Castile, October

Alex owed IV — *Dad? Really, what do I call the man now?* — an answer. While it was entirely unreasonable for anyone to expect him to make a decision about his place in the world within a couple of days, time truly was of the essence here. Pancreatic cancer took its victims quickly and, while the king still had a certain amount of mobility, that could change, permanently, without notice. If IV were going to make an announcement about Alex, it needed to come soon.

Alex had spent hours on the phone with Angélica discussing the pros and cons. Eventually, they'd even brought Allie in on the conversation, swearing her to secrecy. Allie of course thought it was the coolest thing in the world that her father was a prince, even as she was confused over where that left the man she'd always considered her grandfather. She also reiterated – multiple times – how much she loved Léon, even going so far as to say that, while she'd miss her New York friends, she wouldn't mind finishing her education in Castile.

Alex even consulted with Vidente, who admitted that she knew who Alex's real father was all along, but that it wasn't her place to provide this information. Then she suggested to him that ignoring his destiny was dangerous.

"Yes, but who is to say which of these things is my destiny?" he said to his great-great-grandmother. "Maybe I've already been living my destiny all of these years."

"One of the central mysteries, *bisnieto*."

"Aren't you supposed to have some clarity on the central mysteries from your perspective?"

"Whoever told you that?"

In the end, all of these conversations had left him no closer to a decision. He had his family's blessing to go where his heart led him, but that had simply put the choice squarely in his lap, something that wouldn't normally be a problem. Alex had often felt that his decision-making skills were amongst the greatest attributes that had led him to a successful career. But this was only tangentially a business decision, wasn't it? In many ways, the business implications were the easiest to comprehend.

All of this played through his mind as he sat down to breakfast with Fernando. They'd seen each other multiple times since IV broke the news to his son, and Fernando had taken to calling him "brother," which both acknowledged the prince's acceptance and suggested that Fernando no longer felt that he could refer to him as "Alejandro Soberano," as he'd been doing since they'd met. Each time they'd seen each other in recent days, Fernando had suggested more insistently that the royal family was in stasis until Alex let them know his wishes, which brought more portent to each subsequent meeting. The message was obvious: *this can't go on much longer.*

"It dawns on me that it's possible that I haven't been clear," Fernando said before Alex had even had his first sip of coffee. "Being king holds no appeal for me. Maybe education minister. I think that's about the right scale for me. Agree to make me education minister, and we can close this deal right now."

Alex chuckled. "I think you've been abundantly clear about your preferences, Fernando."

"But we haven't truly discussed those preferences since this . . . revelation."

"I'm aware of how you feel about taking the throne."

"Yes, but we've always spoken about it in the context of inevitability. I couldn't refuse the crown, because I couldn't allow it to pass to my impaired brother or my incompetent and maybe criminal cousin. But those aren't the only choices anymore, are they? On his deathbed, the king announces that there's a different heir to the throne. I endorse it with absolute sincerity — something I wouldn't need to fake, by the way — therefore avoiding any controversy. I embrace you as my brother — again something I wouldn't need to fake — and vow to help the new king in any way that I can. You get to be Léon's new superhero — the man who vanquished the despotic Ólgar — and I get to go on with my life, free at last from the burden of eventual ascension."

"What makes you think I have any interest in being 'Léon's new superhero?'"

"Oh, come on. You already gained mythic status during the whole Ólgar thing when they were calling you 'The Assassin.' Are you telling me you didn't enjoy that?"

"No, I didn't enjoy that. There was a group of people who thought I permanently disabled the prime minister. That I'd effectively staged a coup. Some of them still do."

"Not anyone who counts. And even if the rumor persists, it just adds to your legend. You're the anti-General."

Alex had known that Fernando wouldn't fight him over the throne, knew that his friend would delight in stepping away from the responsibility. However, in switching to hard-sell mode, Fernando had prompted a vision for Alex that the prince certainly hadn't intended: a vision of himself being transformed from man to symbol. Attainment of power had always been a significant part of Alex's agenda. Power was one of the primary reasons — though hardly the only one — behind his constant efforts to build his corporation to the level he'd built it and to keep building it. But that was an *active* power, one gained from the tireless quest to help his companies perform. Being "Léon's new superhero" was a very different kind of power, one that would require him to redefine himself on nearly every level. In business, the agenda was clear: you targeted a market and did everything you could to succeed in that market. Politics was another thing entirely. It was all messiness and gray areas, and any part of the agenda could shift on a daily basis. He hadn't trained for this, and he wasn't sure that anyone adapted to this sort of thing well at this stage of adulthood.

It was at this point that several thoughts came together in Alex's mind simultaneously.

"I don't want your father — our father — to acknowledge me as his."

Fernando threw his head back. "Please tell me you're not saying this."

"I'm saying it. I have a life I love in New York. A life doing things I am passionate about doing — things I was *made for.*"

"Well, technically, you were *made* to be king."

"Technically, I don't think I was."

Fernando waved his hand. "There's no point in getting caught up in technicalities. Maybe you're made for this as well."

"I'm not. Seriously. But you know who is? You. Whether you realize it or not, you've been learning how to be king since you were an infant. You've been running away from it for nearly as long, but if you stop running, you could be an enormous asset to your country."

"Because I'm mediagenic?"

"Because you're passionate about things."

"Not about *king* things. The way the government is set up, the palace only has meaningful authority over matters of finance. I have zero interest in matters of finance. If I only knew someone who did . . ."

"Don't deflect. Change the 'king things.' The palace wasn't always focused exclusively on finance. That was your father's doing. Think about it, Fernando. What truly engages you? You know that you were never happier than when you were helping kids learn in Saint-Paul de-Vence. Take the kind of leadership role in education that your father took in Léon's economy. Prove your model here and export it all over the world."

Fernando fixed Alex with a stare that let Alex know that he was processing this. Then he broke eye contact.

"Just one little problem: the prime minister isn't going to neuter the role of minister of education," Fernando said.

"He will if you loosen the palace's reins on finance. Give the prime minister more control over the budget, and he will gladly tell the Minister of Education to give you whatever you want. Either that or he'll replace him with someone who will."

Fernando looked down at his plate and shook his head slowly. "I have a better idea: you become king and I spend the rest of my days on vacation."

"The vacation is over, Fernando," Alex said sharply. "Take this role and do something magnificent with it."

Fernando seemed stricken by Alex's words. Then the prince shook his head slowly and looked off in the middle distance.

"Well, maybe if I'm lucky I'll die young like my father."

"That was overly melodramatic even for you. I'm not finished. It would be wrong for me to become king because I haven't grown into the role and it would be horrible for both Léon and me to have me learning on the job. But just because I don't want to be acknowledged as a Trastámara now doesn't mean that I never want it to happen. Do you know when I want that to happen?"

"When I've become such an embarrassment as a king that the nation is ready for literally anyone else?"

"Let's assume that you're going to stop saying things like that as soon as this breakfast is over." Alex paused, giving himself a few more seconds to make sure that he truly believed that what he was about to suggest was right for all involved. "No, the time when I want the world to know that I am a Trastámara is when Allie turns thirty — the day she becomes queen."

Fernando's eyes grew so wide that Alex wondered if the man's eyebrows were going to leap from his head.

"Now you have my attention," the prince said.

There was no more equivocation in Alex's mind. "This is still coming to me, so bear with me. The second Allie stepped on Léon's soil she fell in love with this country. Allie has traveled well in her young life, but I've never seen her react to a place like this before. On top of this, if we truly learned anything during the Ólgar affair, it's that my daughter has an ability to deal with pressure that few her age can match. And she has skills she exhibited during the Ólgar incident that I think it's safe to say make her one in a million. No, one in a *billion.* One can only imagine how remarkable she could become if she were exposed to statecraft at a young age."

"And how do we arrange such exposure?"

"Allie will summer here. You'll expose her to more and more every summer. Then she'll spend her last two years of high school in Léon before getting her degree at Harvard and then putting in a couple of years at my company to round her out. After that, you'll give her a significant role within the palace that will provide her with all of the finishing she needs. This, of course, is contingent on her agreeing to all of this."

"She's eleven years old. Are eleven-year-olds capable of comprehending this grand plan you're devising?"

"We'll put the rest of the plan in place with your father now, and we'll hold off on the discussion with Allie until we feel she's ready to comprehend it. Maybe that will be years from now. Maybe it'll be next week. She's a very polished kid. And we both know she has remarkable talents."

Fernando laughed, and Alex at first thought that his friend was going to mock Alex's grand plan. But when Fernando stopped laughing, what came across his face was an expression of relief.

"So, when she turns thirty, we hold a press conference, I abdicate, we reveal who you and Allie really are, and she becomes queen?"

"And you get to enjoy a retirement filled with exotic travel, speaking engagements with outrageously high fees, and, oh, endless awards from countries all around the world for the contributions you've made to revolutionizing education. And let me be clear about that: you *are* going to revolutionize education. It is the gift you were meant to give the world, and you're not allowed to keep it to yourself. If you do, I will let you die a king. Allie will be quite happy and fulfilled running my company instead."

Fernando smiled bemusedly. "This is an insane scenario, you realize. Though my children would come to thank me for it, I'm sure. I can't imagine they want the throne any more than I do."

"That's very possibly true. And, really is this any more insane than my suddenly being announced as the true heir?"

"It might be, actually."

Alex leaned toward his dear friend and brother. "Think about it. Really think about it. Everyone fulfills a key role in this scenario."

"Everyone except for you. You just get to go back to New York and continue being a mogul. I saw what you did there."

Alex laughed. "I wasn't completely finished. Here's the rest. You name me financial advisor to the king. Even if you're going to turn most of the budget over to the prime minister, you're going to want someone with a vested interest looking at all of the numbers and making sure the prime minister isn't being sloppy – or, you know, building up a huge war chest to launch an invasion of Portugal."

"Please don't even joke about that sort of thing. Okay, the financial advisor position makes sense. And it also makes it easier to justify Allie's presence here every summer. And with you next to me, I can easily fake it."

"That too."

Fernando laughed. It was the first unforced laugh Alex had heard from him during this trip to Léon.

"I always knew I loved you, brother. But if I had anticipated this scenario, I would have loved you even more. You've always managed to save me from myself, and now you're doing it again."

"I'd prefer to believe that I've just been reminding you who you really are."

"We'll leave that for history to decide. But I'll tell you this, Alejandro Soberano: I'm going to try being the person that *you* see rather than the person that *I* see for a while. Who knows? You might even see better than I do."

Fernando locked eyes with Alex and once again shook his head from side to side. This time, however, not in resignation. "I certainly hadn't anticipated this breakfast going in this direction."

Chapter 18
Castile, December

Sandra flew to Léon with Alex and his family. Things had been awkward between herself and her son for about a week after his return to New York, but they talked it through and got to the other side of it. Since the morning Cayetano and she had broken the news to Alex, she'd been debating with herself over waiting so long to let him know. Had she hurt him by doing so? Was the opposite true? Was there some way she could have handled this differently without harming others? Sandra understood that asking these questions now had little value, but she also had a feeling she would be asking them many times in the future.

She chose not to go to the coronation. She'd spent a good deal of time with her family yesterday. Allie seemed particularly excited about taking her to a place where beautiful flowers grew, even at this time of year. The sense of wonder in the girl's eyes, even though the king's death had saddened her, was rich emotional nourishment for Sandra, something she especially appreciated right now.

And today, she went to the church by herself, even though Alex encouraged her to come to the private viewing being held for the king's closest and dearest. She felt that she needed to do this alone. And while she knew she was most likely closer and dearer to Cayetano than anyone who attended the private viewing, that was something best kept to herself, especially in this moment.

There were thousands of people waiting in the chapel for an opportunity to say goodbye to their king. The people of Léon had created a vision in their collective consciousness of Alfonso IV as a compassionate, strong, wise, and approachable leader who was a staunch defender of those he presided over. None of the people standing in the queue with her — not the husband and wife with their two small children in front of her, nor the softly weeping woman in her seventies behind her, nor any of the others — knew that she could confirm that vision for them. King Alfonso IV had been all of those things, and Cayetano Trastámara had been even more: deeply empathetic, generously loving, a wonderful companion. If she'd been in the position to eulogize the man, she would have shared all of this with everyone assembled. And she would have kept some other things entirely to herself, because they were meant only for she and Cayetano to own together.

As she got closer to the front of the line, she could see the royal family sitting dutifully by the side of the casket. Even Cayetano's two grandchildren, who he doted on until the last of his strength gave out. Even the troubled son whose drug problems had caused Cayetano so much worry over the years. Sandra had never met Cayetano's wife, for obvious reasons, but she had met Fernando, now King Fernando I, on a number of occasions when he came to New York to see Alex. It was possible he would recognize her when she knelt to say goodbye to his father, but Sandra knew he wouldn't acknowledge this in any way. Not today, at least.

Alex might have been sitting with the royal family as well if he'd chosen differently. Sandra had no quarrel with his decision, though it meant that Cayetano had gone to his grave — and likely she would as well — without the truth being revealed in anything other than sealed papers. Alex made the decision that was right for him and the people he loved. And the fact that less than two decades from now her little playmate of a granddaughter would be monarch of this nation tickled Sandra even in these somber surroundings.

Sandra was now at the front of the line, and it was time for her to stand before the casket. She knew she would only have a moment here. She had so much to say to Cayetano, but this was not the place to say those things. And she'd already been saying them to him in her own way since she learned of his death two days ago.

She knelt and looked at the physical remains of the man she loved like no one else. He continued to seem regal even though his soul had moved on. Regal enough to command the room one last time.

"We fulfilled every bit of that promise," she said in a whisper.

As she rose to step down, she found that her legs were giving her a bit of trouble. That's when she felt a hand at her elbow, helping her to rise. It was Fernando.

"I want to thank you," the king said. "For everything."

She smiled at him warmly. "All of it was love, and none of it was effort."

He wiped at his eyes. "The first time I've cried over him."

Sandra felt her own tears coming. "You'll do him proud, Your Majesty. He always believed in you. I don't know if you ever knew this, Fernando, but he felt the same way as you did when he became king, and look how well he did. He would have been perfectly happy if he'd never become king, if his family had never been returned to the throne. He had many other ambitions. I might be the only person alive now who knows this."

"Instead, he took his rightful place and returned Léon to greatness." Fernando wiped at his eyes again and then looked directly into Sandra's eyes. "I will keep the kingdom great for your granddaughter, and one day she will be the wisest and most important queen in Europe."

"I wish I could be around to see that. But I will enjoy watching your reign for as long as I get to witness it. You're going to be a fine king, Fernando. Your father knew that, and I know it."

Then she patted his arm and stepped down from the altar.

◊ ◊ ◊

Castile, December

Alex enjoyed watching Fernando speak. He'd of course seen his friend give interviews many times in the past, and in all of those Fernando projected the personality he'd cultivated: the clever, carefree, disengaged royal who was much more likely to respond at length to a bit of European gossip than to any question related to the state of the nation for which he was a prince. The Fernando at the podium now still projected cleverness and wit, but he was sharing something with the public here that Alex had not witnessed in earlier meetings with the press: empathy. In his first major press conference since his coronation, King Fernando I – in classic Fernando fashion, he'd decided to use his own name as his royal name – had shown a surprising grasp of the issues that faced his country and, more importantly, the concerns that the people of Léon had. His responses to questions about the nation's high unemployment rate, the disenfranchisement of some immigrant communities, and rising drug addiction and alcoholism rates showed an appreciation for these issues that no briefing book could have provided him. Of course, he became most passionate when talking about a series of initiatives he hoped to bring to the country's schools in the coming year. The minister of education had agreed to step aside in January to allow the prime minister – and, really, Fernando – to choose a replacement more closely aligned to the new king's ideas. The minister had landed firmly on his feet as, after a brief consultancy, he would become the new dean of the University of Aragon, one of Léon's elite institutions.

Alex was seated to the left of the podium with the prime minister to his left and the minister of finance to his right. Alex had had reservations about Fernando announcing his role so soon after his coronation. After all, even though none of the media knew that Alex and Fernando shared the same father, most of them knew that the two of them had shared a long friendship. Alex was concerned that Fernando might be perceived as putting together an "old boy's network," and of filling his team with his drinking buddies, but Fernando strongly believed that letting the country know that Alex was on the team would project solidity. Alex attempted to debate this, but he quickly learned that King Fernando's resolve was considerably greater than Prince Fernando's had been.

"I'm delighted to let you know that my father's chief of staff has agreed to stay on in that capacity," Fernando said to the assemblage. "I cannot express clearly enough how much of a relief this is to me. Not only is Victor one of the keenest political minds in the world, but he also has surprising powers of persuasion with the palace's kitchen staff, and it is good to know that, as we're putting in very late hours, we will at least be eating well."

Fernando threw a casual salute toward the much older COS, who nodded in appreciation.

"I'm also very happy to announce that Isabella Prodigio has agreed to come on as my deputy chief of staff. Many of you know Isabella from the numerous 'thirty under thirty' pieces that have been written about her the last few years, but I promise you're going to be hearing much more from her. When the prime minister learned that Isabella was willing to leave the private sector, he nearly wept because he'd missed out on his chance to bring her onto his team."

The prime minister offered a self-deprecating smile while Isabella – a woman Alex guessed might someday occupy the prime minister's office – stood and waved.

"Finally, I wanted to let you know that my dear friend Alejandro Soberano has agreed to work with the palace as special financial advisor to the king without compensation. As many of you know, Alex is my closest friend. He was also a trusted confidante of my father's and is of course a brilliant businessman. Some of the reporters in the back of the room might have written some speculation about Alex this year, but I can promise you that our current prime minister feels entirely safe around him."

Fernando gestured toward Alex, who stood up to wave to the assemblage.

A reporter raised his hand and Fernando took the question as Alex sat down.

"Your Majesty, did anyone ever mention to you that you and Mr. Soberano look like brothers?"

Alex felt his blood pressure spike, but a quick glance at Fernando showed him that the king had not lost his composure.

"I'm flattered that you think I look as good as Alex does, though I suppose you didn't actually say that. Alex is as close as a brother to me, and we've known each other a long time. Perhaps we're like an old married couple who start to look like one another after all of those years."

The reporters laughed, and Fernando took a few more questions before ending the press conference.

◊ ◊ ◊

Two days later, Alex, Angélica, and Allie got ready for their flight back to New York. Mamá had left directly after the funeral, saying she felt too conspicuous to stay for the press conference. That was silly, of course, because virtually no one in Léon knew who his mother was, and far fewer knew of her relationship with IV. Alex had learned a long time ago, though, that tussling with his mother over matters of the heart was a futile exercise.

Allie, on the other hand, didn't want to leave at all. Given her remarkable, perhaps even singular, gifts, had she been aware of what this country meant to her future from the moment she stepped foot on its soil? Alex and Angélica did not intend to share their plans for her until she was old enough to understand them and even reject them if she chose, but did Allie *already* know?

"So, you'll be coming back here once a month, right?" she said as they were getting into the car that would take them to the airport.

"For a few days each month, yes."

"So that means that I can come back here once a month."

"Well, there's that little matter of school. We took you out for this, but I think your teachers might have a bit of a problem with your missing days every month."

"We've had this conversation before, Dad."

"We have. I'm getting the impression, though, that you heard that conversation differently than I heard it."

"You know, someone told me that people's memories get weaker as they get older."

"Very funny. You and Mom can come with me on my summer trips. And maybe we'll have Christmas in Castile next year. That would be fun, wouldn't it?"

"Christmas is only two weeks away now. We *could* have Christmas in Castile this year."

Alex hugged his daughter close to him. Christmas in Castile would be a regular part of the Soberano calendar very soon. And someday, Allie would deliver the holiday message that Fernando would be delivering in a dozen days. Yes, Angélica and he would give Allie every opportunity to reject the plans they had set in motion for her. But as the car headed to the airport and Alex watched his daughter staring out the window wistfully, he knew that she never would.

About the Authors

Julian Iragorri lives in Manhattan. He has worked on Wall Street since the early nineties.

Lou Aronica is the author of the *USA Today* bestseller *The Forever Year* and the national bestseller *Blue*. He also collaborated on the *New York Times* nonfiction bestsellers *The Element* and *Finding Your Element* (with Ken Robinson) and the national bestsellers *The Culture Code* (with Clotaire Rapaille) and *The Greatest You* (with Trent Shelton). Aronica is a long-term book publishing veteran. He is President and Publisher of the independent publishing house The Story Plant. You can reach him at laronica@fictionstudio.com.